THE BOYS

THE BOYS

Toni Sala

*Translated from the Catalan
by Mara Faye Lethem*

Two Lines Press

Els nois © 2014 by Toni Sala Isern
Original edition published by L'Altra Editorial
Translation © 2015 by Mara Faye Lethem

Published by Two Lines Press
582 Market Street, Suite 700, San Francisco, CA 94104
www.twolinespress.com

ISBN 978-1-931883-49-8

Library of Congress Control Number: 2015942169

Design by Ragina Johnson
Cover design by Gabriele Wilson
Cover photo by Christophe Darbelet / Millennium Images, UK

Printed in the United States of America

This project is supported in part by an award from
the National Endowment for the Arts.

ART WORKS.
arts.gov

This book was translated with the help of a grant from
the Institut Ramon Llull.

institut
ramon llull
Catalan Language and Culture

THE BOYS

I

Now it seems we blame everything on the recession, but the recession wasn't to blame for the display of prostitutes out on the shoulder of the highway, out past the halted construction meant to split it in two, past the half-built bridges with faded circus posters and the spray-painted words N-II HIGHWAY OF SHAME, DIVIDE IT ALREADY, past that stretch of highway with its sketchy mirror version, unpaved and separated by a low wall of concrete blocks, past fields flooded by black water and crowned with shocks of grass . . .

The recession wasn't to blame for that display case filled with fresh meat, a whore every hundred meters; the recession wasn't to blame, because the whores were there before—it was during the years filled with cranes that the business extended like an oil spill. But morality doesn't move as fast as money and, with the good years behind them, the girls were still there, resigned like the rest of us to the hardships of the new times.

Club Diana announced the beginning of the display as

you travel north on the national, before you get to Tordera. Fifteen kilometers later, on the outskirts of Vidreres, a similar building—another old block of rooms at the foot of the highway, the Club Margarita—presaged the end. They were the landmarks at each extreme. Despite the distance and mountains that separated them, at night, when their neon signs came on, it seemed the two buildings spoke to each other in a code of blinking lights. On the roof of Club Diana a yellow arrow lit up, flying right into a red pubic triangle; on the roof of Club Margarita a giant daisy lost its petals, one by one, until it suddenly bloomed again among the dark fields.

And there had to be some relationship between the two brothels, because in the Club Margarita parking lot he often saw vans advertising Club Diana: the silhouette of a naked girl dancing on the circles of a bull's-eye. He always passed the brothels in the daytime, when they were still closed—the blinds were always lowered, but he could tell from the deserted parking lots—and the girls, perhaps the same ones who worked in the clubs at night, waited by the side of every road that led to the national highway, sometimes sitting on plastic chairs, with parasols in the summer and umbrellas in the winter or if it was raining. When they were busy they left a towel and a rock on the white plastic chair so it wouldn't move. When they weren't, they talked on their cell phones and smoked with the patience of fishermen on a riverbank until some driver flipped on his turn signal, negotiated a price with the girl from his car, and then took her along the dirt road to behind the first trees, or sometimes not even that far: then he'd see the stopped car and the back of a man's neck through the window, facing away from the highway.

He had seen every make of car stop, vans, trucks, trailers, and motorcycles, and once he saw a black guy walking toward the trees with one hand on his bicycle and the other around a girl's waist.

Yet the girls all seemed cut from the same cloth, none of them older than twenty, all attractive and always wearing makeup, with clean, combed hair, snugly fitting party clothes, and naked from the waist down to their boots at the slightest hint of sunshine. He would see them after lunch on his way back to work, and from the way he studied them he surely knew them better than even their clients. When there were new girls—because the bosses changed them often—they would tempt him with a wink. He'd smile back and, if he was in the mood, he'd blow a kiss, and then he'd wonder if that was taking advantage of the girl, or if she'd understood it as the sign of affection and solidarity that it was, if, deep down, it really even was that at all. The one thing he knew for sure was that they cursed him when they saw he wasn't stopping.

The gesture lasted as long as it took his car to pass by them, like a reminder of youth and the joys of the flesh. He was nearing sixty years old. Did he want something more? Did he desire those bodies? How could he know? They were girls like any others but, luckily, the distance between their lives was vast. Was it better that they were out in the open, or should they be forced to work hidden away? It wasn't good for people to get used to dehumanizing girls, but wasn't having to see them a good punishment? When his girls were little, if they were ever sitting in the back seat when he had to go down those fifteen kilometers of sex on display, he made sure not to take his eyes off the license plate of the car in front of him, not out of shame, but to ward off the jolts life brings.

Past the Tordera Bridge, the highway lost its sea views and climbed behind the backs of Blanes and Lloret until, after a blind hill, it opened up on the plain of La Selva, with the luminous teeth of the Pyrenees in the background.

He'd traveled that route every day for the last fifteen years, ever since they'd transferred him to a small branch of the Santander Bank in Vidreres. He knew it better than the back of his hand: the patched highway, the ghost gas stations and warehouses, the large rusty silo, the trees with sawed branches whose trunks almost touched the asphalt, the descent to the plain of La Selva, and Vidreres like a tiny island among the fields, with an antique tractor and a Catalan flag at the traffic circle as you enter, and a small spiderweb of streets and people. He knew what he had to know about the town where he earned his living, which family each client belonged to, who had money and who didn't and who someday might, who was important in town hall and who wasn't, that sort of thing. He used the slow, gentle accent of the local dialect when speaking with them, aware that he would always be an outsider there, no matter how many years he spent working right across from the Santa Maria church at a job in which he was privy to more of the town's secrets than the rector himself, or even the girls at Club Margarita.

Money moves between men like a gust of wind. In a small town, where the amount of money is always the same, you can watch it just move from one account to another like birds changing branches. That was the only appeal of the job, watching the deposits and withdrawals, the incoming salaries and the unexpected expenses, those intimate movements of money—he had access to private spaces. He controlled the movements in the bankbooks, the investments, the gambles, the timed deposits, the pension plans, the mortgages, and the loans. He and his coworker speculated on where the money came from and where it was headed. Nothing surprised him. They foretold which businesses would do well or go under; they worked in the most predictable office in the world, with the most conservative clientele on the planet, and, even still, it was fun.

He reached the office as the bell tower rang eight o'clock, as usual. His colleague was from the town—sometimes it was like having the enemy in your home—but they were the same age, which is similar to being born in the same place.

He let his coworker raise the shutter and pick up the newspaper, as he did every day. This time he just stood at the door and turned the pages until he found the news he was looking for.

"Heaven help us," he said, and gave a whistle. "What a sight."

Ernest looked over his colleague's shoulder at the newspaper. A photograph showed a black Peugeot with the hood crunched and the windshield shattered. The radiator grille had come off and the engine was beside the car, because it had fallen out in the accident. They had carried it separately to the municipal morgue where they took the photograph. Two brothers die in an accident in Vidreres. The savage jolt that, only through some miracle of elasticity, avoids ripping apart the spiderweb of a family or an entire town.

Jaume was shaking his head.

"They drive like madmen," he said. "I'm surprised more of them don't get themselves killed."

You wouldn't say that if the dead boys were your sons, thought Ernest.

During the first few hours on a Monday, Vidreres is still warming up, few people come into the office, and you can spend a good chunk of the morning watching the other side of the street from your desk: the little paved square with four benches and four clipped trees, dry parterres, and the large door to the Santa Maria church.

The reinforced glass of the branch's windows scarcely echoed the vibration of the few cars that circulated on the pedestrian street. They had modernized the town center four years earlier. People from the outlying areas of Barcelona bought places in the housing complexes, and Vidreres grew the way all towns near highway exits do. But the town center continued to have the same families as ever, and every morning from behind the glass he saw the same soundproofed women heading toward the bakery and the butcher's shop. Hourglasses with baskets, little figures in a clock dragging the shadows, sundials. At ten on the nose, Mrs. Garcés passed by. Five minutes later, Marta came out of her house. Five seconds after that, Mrs. Dolors turned the corner. They stopped to greet each other, following an ancestral routine, commenting on the television programs they'd seen the day before. From their gestures he guessed at whether Enriqueta's bones were aching that morning or not. Mr. Vidal railed against the politicians: "The young people are right to protest! Just you wait until they get fed up! Just you wait!" Miquel Sr. warned of some clouds coming from Girona with a nod of his head. They had farming in their blood. They never missed the weather report.

That morning, the conversations went on longer than usual. Heads shook and hands opened. Miquel Sr., who usually read the newspaper at the community social club, carried it under his arm. If they hadn't thought to order more for the kiosk, the local papers would sell out. Into the silence of the sun and winter frost, in a corner of the office, at low volume, Radio Vidreres repeated the news of Saturday's accident every hour. The host spoke in a thin voice, and without naming names he announced that the funeral was that afternoon.

"Why do they have to keep going on about the accident," grumbled Jaume.

He wore black shoes, black pants, black tie, dark shirt.

"Are you going to the funeral?" asked Ernest.

On the street there was also a lot of dark clothing.

"Don't expect any clients."

"Did you know them?"

"Everyone knew them. The only sons in the Batlle family, over in Les Serres. Their father works for La Caixa bank. Did you see the marks?"

"What marks?"

"I'm surprised you didn't notice them on your way in. You can still see the skid marks on the asphalt."

Then Mr. Cals came in, like he did every Monday at that time, to take out fifty euros. There's no way Mr. Cals, who was retired, lived on so little, especially since they saw him pass by the office every day with a small lit cigar. But every Monday he came to get his fifty-euro note and didn't come back for the rest of the week. Once the water and electricity bills were paid, the rest of his pension piled up in his account. Today he was dressed in mourning clothes that were out of style and had been ironed too many times. He gave off the scent of mothballs and his shoes were shiny. Ernest remembered the suit as the same one he wore at his wife's funeral.

"You see, Jaume, that's life," said Mr. Cals. "Twenty, twenty-one years old? And what are they gonna do at Can Batlle without those boys? Goddamn it all to hell, isn't that just the way it is. Those poor people. Who could've ever even imagined such a thing! Now it's Lluís's moment. I told him, I did. Wait, be patient, life takes many twists and turns, holy hell does it ever. Twenty million he offered them, fifteen years back! Twenty million pesetas, twenty years ago! Let's see what old Batlle can get for that land now. I already told him: you, now, keep quiet as a mouse. Lucky bastard. You can just imagine the party going on yesterday at the Margarita, goddamn it to hell."

Mr. Cals put the banknote in his wallet and the wallet in his pocket. He couldn't stop talking.

"I'm old and don't care about anything now; otherwise, if I were twenty years younger, maybe that bastard Lluís wouldn't be fast enough and I'd get the land. He can shove it up his ass. When you see these tragedies you say fuck it all, man, come on, to hell with it all, shit, to hell with all of it, and God and his virgin mother, fuck, I wouldn't want to be in Batlle's shoes right now, holy hell, or Llúcia's, because that's some real bad luck, both sons, goddamn it, both of them, holy shit. And where were those poor kids coming from so early in the morning?... I guess I'll be seeing you later, holy fuck, goddamn, shit, holy shit, fucking hell."

He left the office cursing.

"Boy, is he mad!" said Jaume. "He can see it coming. Lluís is going to buy up the lands of Can Batlle. It's killing Cals. He's obsessed with land. Don't you see he's still saving up? I don't think he has enough. He's got some, but not that much. And with today's prices... Or maybe he does have the dough, and that's why he's been telling the other guy to keep quiet and wait. We still might get a surprise. You never know with these old guys. Maybe he has an account in Andorra or a fortune under his floor tiles. I know him all too well; I've had to put up with him all my life. When I was a kid we walked past his field on the way to school, and we were all scared of him. He would be digging, and he'd look up and wouldn't bend over again until we were gone. And there wasn't even anything there for us to touch. Just a fig tree by the road, the one that's still there."

On the other side of the glass, the square was filling up. Mourners arrived from every street. It didn't seem like there were this many people in Vidreres, a little town where the streets were always pretty much empty—in summer because of the heat off the plain and now in the winter because of the cold air from the Montseny and the Pyrenees and sometimes the fog. He was no longer listening to his coworker. Jaume was going on and on about the old man's stinginess, as if the time had come to account for the debts of an entire lifetime. It was the swarm of words that death attracts, and Ernest let him talk, trying not to listen, until he couldn't take it anymore and cut him off: "Do you really think today's the day to be talking about that?"

His coworker let a moment pass before standing up. No one likes to be told they're petty. When you speak of petty things it's because you want your interlocutor to join in, you are offering him a bit of freedom from his prison of niceties. When you open that door to invite him to share in your baseness, when you are standing there, exposed to the elements, it's not pleasant to be reminded that not everyone is from the town, that there are outsiders who only come in to work and who remain unsullied by local misfortunes. Ernest could understand that and forgive Jaume, even return the favor and invite him to the party of his own lowliness, continuing the exchange of small, everyday evils as if nothing had happened. After all, they were people of transactions—they knew how to play with prices and stock values. It was precisely because they understood each other that his repugnance was so strong. Jaume could have gotten violent, he could have scuttled all the things on the desk onto the floor, picked up the letter opener and threatened him, asked him who he thought he was. But he just said, "I'm going to the funeral."

And he went to the closet, resolutely and silently. It was worse than physical violence; it was as if he shouted: You think you've taught me some big lesson, but I'm the one going to the funeral, not you. Me, I'm from here. You don't have even the slightest idea of what's going on. You're an outsider. I'm from here and so are my parents and my wife and my children. So just shut up. You think you have the simplicity of those dead boys in your favor. Well, here's something else that's simple: I am in mourning, I will go to the funeral, I will share in the town's grief, I will be with them, I will cry with them. I'm dying to cry with them. Just wait, you'll see what a big crowd there'll be. We won't all fit into the church. Look at the square. The whole high school is there. The soccer team. The parade association. Those boys' friends. You see the young people? You see the old fogeys? We'll all be there. We'll flood the church with tears. And the church isn't more than two hundred meters from this office. I'll have to wipe my feet before I come back in. I will be there and you will be here, doing numbers and thinking about your daughters. Go to hell. You stay here to watch over the office in case some other outsider like you comes in. I'll be there, listening to the mass with the others. I'll hear the wails of their parents and friends, the sobs echoing against the church walls as they have for a thousand years, me and everyone else will be buried there among the dead, it will be a physical thing and not one of your jokes, I will be there with my people and you here adding up numbers, waiting, and contemplating. That's the truth and not your moralizing. Save your morality for the day your daughters are killed. Then we'll see if you still feel like giving lessons.

He was used to hearing the bells toll for the dead and watching funerals from the bank office, but this time, alone behind the desk, as the church door swallowed up the swarm of people, he had the impression that the bells tolled louder than ever, twice as loud, four, eight times louder, because there were two boys dead and Jaume had left him alone in the office. They came through the glass with such intensity.

They rang so loud. Why such immodesty? Did they have to tell everyone that the boys had finally reached the moment of knowing everything, of seeing everything, of understanding their own existence completely? Did it have to be shouted from the rooftops? We spend our lives in retreat, only at the bottom of the well can we know if life was worth living or not, or, to put it better even though it's the same thing: only then can we know whether we can know if life was worth living. But we can't communicate that knowledge. Why toll the bells? To remind him that, when the moment comes, his death will also serve to torment others?

He searched for Mr. Cals amid the crowd in the square. He tried to figure out who Lluís could be. He looked for his coworker's wife and children. He recognized clients. The host of Radio Vidreres must have been there as well, because only music was heard on that bandwidth.

Once everyone was inside the church, the first hearse was able to enter the square, backing up to the doors. Two funeral home employees dressed like businessmen unloaded the first coffin. They went up the steps and put it on a metal platform with wheels. The empty car moved aside, and the second car entered the square.

Inside the church they waited for the dead with the same expectation they would have for a bride and groom. Which brother was in which box? Did they have little plaques with their names, or was that not necessary? We live fighting against randomness: there has to be a protocol. Would it be the older brother who entered the church first—first to arrive, first to leave? The same employees carried out the same task. Afterward, the second car left the church door and parked beside the other one, in the middle of the square.

He switched off the radio. He wanted some excuse to call home. He let the feeling pass through him, the way he let mornings in the office pass. He didn't want to turn himself into a bell tower. It was sunny, no one was left on the street, the kiosk and the bakery were shuttered. He thought of the priest, the poor guy, having to serve as a hinge, having to speak when there's nothing to say. He thought of that little man he watched go in and out of the church each day, thought of his self-censure, of his self-control, of a priest's forced cerebral mutilation, of his sacrifice for his parish, his loyalty to lies and ritual. Unless he was a con man and lived off others' weakness.

Most people hadn't gone to the wake, but some of them, the closest relatives, had. They had seen the boys displayed in their two coffins, humiliated like stuffed animals in the double zoo of their death: caged by rigor mortis and caged by the glass-topped coffins. Or perhaps it was their victory, their revenge, and it is the dead that watch over us.

And then he heard an engine approaching the square, a truck, it had to be from somewhere else, on that day, and it was already strange that it was squeezing its way down such narrow streets. He approached the door to watch it pass. It was carrying a load of hay bales. Bales of hay in January. You saw them going back and forth in June and July, after the harvest, or in the months following, but never at this time of year... They were the old style of bales, rectangular and small; someone must have ordered them for the animals they kept, they must be coming from Llagostera or Cassà, the truck driver was confused, he was looking for someone to ask what was going on, where were the owners of the house where he was scheduled to drop them off, why had he found it locked . . .

When he saw that he'd reached the church square, the driver put the truck in neutral in the middle of the street and got out of the cab. He was a tall man, about thirty years old, with short hair and a Van Dyke beard, and the strong body of a young hauler. He had bits of straw stuck in his blue sweater. Ernest half hid behind a column, and the truck driver looked toward the closed bakery and kiosk not understanding a thing. He checked his watch and then walked slowly over to the community social club. The door was open. He found the place empty except for Cindy, the South American girl who worked behind the bar. She must have explained to him what was going on, must have told him he should park and have a coffee while the funeral finished, because after a second the truck driver left the club, got into the cab, and parked down the street.

They died so young they took the whole town's life with them, the trucker must have thought. He hadn't parked in Vidreres, he'd parked in the Vidreres cemetery, with niches like houses; a cemetery with a kiosk, a bakery, and a bank; a cemetery with streets, with a church; a cemetery with a cemetery; with a club and a parking lot filled with empty cars. That's what the afterlife must be like: solitude and walls.

Meanwhile, the priest spoke, and no one took their eyes off the two coffins, placed perpendicular to the altar at Christ's feet. And while the entire town of Vidreres, locked up tight in the church, struggled not to imagine the dead brothers' bodies, their faces, while they all tried to shrug off their curiosity, tried not to want to know what clothes the poor saps were wearing, nor who'd had to decide on the shirts the boys would wear to their own funeral and pull them out of the closet... Who had chosen the pants, the socks, the shoes, which weren't their usual Sunday morning shoes but imposter shoes, an attempt to fool them, to pretend that perhaps they could warm their feet, as it should be in a tolerable world where parents died before their children... The pretense dignified the shoes, made them useful in their attempt to console, because useless objects are monstrous; he was sick of seeing it at the bank, money rotting in the vaults and creating bad blood between relatives... But, at the moment of truth, the shoes made the cadavers more contemptible, because death won the match, infecting the clothes and the coffins, infecting the church and all of Vidreres with its ugliness. Not even the consolation trick worked. When he got home each day, the first thing Ernest wanted to do was loosen the laces and take off his shoes... and those shoes would last longer than the feet they were on. Meanwhile, in the church, no one wanted to know who had pulled them out of the closet, whether it was their mother, their aunt, or their father, all three of whom were sitting in the front row with their backs to everyone and facing the coffins, contaminated; no one wanted to imagine the expression on the face that handed over the boys' changes of clothes, in a bag, to the man at the funeral home, a last package for the brothers, sent to hell... They had given the boys' clothes—not new, not bought for the occasion, but already worn, already lived in, to a stranger, a man they'd never seen before, and that stranger put on some gloves and stuffed cotton into the boys' noses and ears and then, with another stranger, stood the dead boys up, first one then the other, to dress them, and the boys stood like plastic dolls, and those strangers at the funeral home were now standing as well, behind the last bench, with their gazes on everyone's backs, supervising the ceremony, waiting to take the coffins away again, because the coffins were theirs, they would always be, a dead man owns nothing . . . Those strangers would be the last ones to have seen and touched the brothers' bodies. And while some inside the church tried to respect the memory of the dead . . . how does one respect a memory? How can you think about a dead man without mucking him up? How can you separate him from the living? While at the church they tried not to curse the brothers for what they represented: death before its time, the most absolute, double death, because an unexpected death is a death that doubles back on itself, that kills hope and longing, that doesn't leave time for making plans or for renouncing making plans, it is a death that doesn't let death live, doesn't let it make a will, or project anything for what's left of life; it kills the future like any death but also kills all possible expectations and therefore kills the past, a retroactive death, a death that shoots at itself from the future, that overtakes death, that passes it, the death of death itself, a death that commits suicide . . . While the adults rummaged through memories to make an inventory of what remained of the two boys—what images, which smiles, what residue they had left behind—they found some surprises, because, now that they were dead, the last time they saw the two brothers became the last time they would ever see the two brothers, and the memory grew laden with nostalgia for what they now knew had been about to happen the last time they saw them. And the smiling faces of the brothers, who couldn't imagine what awaited them. And the last words they said now meant different things, and therefore required a different answer from those who knew the future, a rectification from the prophets... And while they relived those last moments, they remembered how they themselves were at the brothers' ages, what they were doing at the ages the brothers would remain, and they compared the two, and then they calculated what they would have missed out on if they had died young like them, and they tried not to cheat and decide whether living beyond their youth had been worth the effort, and finding that it had, they decided that against the brothers, and it was like spitting on them... and while some looked at each other out of the corners of their eyes, searching for how to behave, how to find the right tone—not too affected or too cold over the abandonment, over the novelty of it—they found it was impossible to avoid hypocrisy, and they gave thanks for the conventions, the ritual, the priest who didn't allow them to start shouting or dancing or to burn down the church... While they did that, at the bank Ernest thought that even though those boys were from Vidreres and their fathers, mother, grandparents, and an endless line of ancestors were from Vidreres, given the way things had turned out, those two boys were the least from Vidreres of anyone on the planet right now, less than the last grain of sand in the depths of the sea. And while inside the church the more emotional people cried, the hearses waited outside, parked in the middle of the square, breaking the law. Keys hung serenely from car locks, the policemen were at mass, and the truck driver had a coffee at the bar with Cindy in the large, empty club with its high ceiling, marble tables, and the television talking to itself; meanwhile, in the Santander Bank branch, standing behind the glass, Ernest focused on the strands of hay that had fallen off the bales on the truck. They were at the foot of the wheels and on the sidewalk, hollow strands of straw, and a slight gust of wind dragged them up and down, from one corner of the square to the other, and when the sun hit them they sparkled, splattered, gilded the whirling air with ephemeral cornucopias.

II

He drove slowly, searching for the site of the accident. He saw the girl by the side of the highway. She didn't look familiar at all. Thin, childlike, with long curly hair and bright eyes, stuffed into a tight little white dress, a bottle of water in one hand and a cell phone in the other. He could have touched her if he stuck his hand out the car window.

He had been thinking about the two brothers' deaths all morning, and now he was tired. One enters the adult world through death's door, through the assumption of mysteries, the most simple and fantastic mysteries of life and death. Being an adult is accepting death, harboring it inside you like a cancer, dying. How can he accept that his own daughters are already adults, that they are already infected? Accept death, how could he? How can you accept something you don't understand? How can you continue to be a person if you accept the incomprehensible? Accepting death is accepting loneliness, and his turmoil over the death of the two brothers was, in fact, his resistance to facing up to his own age, to his own death, resistance to separating from his daughters, the death of his daughters—by dying, the brothers had freed their parents from killing them, as he would have to kill his daughters the day he died. He'd had them too old, almost forty. He'd made up his mind late, with a younger wife. Now he was living in immaturity, on the uncomfortable border between two worlds. He traveled to the world of his daughters, but what if they had actually grown up so much that they were no longer there? Was there even anyone left in this world he had fallen into?

He passed the girl. The Pyrenees, the Guilleries, and the Montseny mountains suddenly appeared in view. They were experiencing the initial cold as autumn turned to winter, with lunar ice, a smattering of grays, and impotent patches of sun. The highway bound the fields together like a ribbon of grief. The tall plane trees were the feathers of a buried monster, the fins of transparent fish that fed on the earth like parasites. Two solitary poplars in the middle of a field represented the two brothers' skeletons, wedged into the earth and touching each other with their branches.

It happened here, right before him. The asphalt was striped with tire marks. The brothers had braked before hitting the tree. They hadn't had an entirely treacherous death. The fierce screech had flown over the fields, appearing on the streets of Vidreres with such violence that the next day the townspeople found tire tracks in the hallways of their homes, on their sofas, in their showers, on their sheets.

Why had they slammed on the brakes? Had an animal crossed their path? Was a car coming at them head-on? Had the brother who was driving nodded off, then woken up suddenly and tried to avoid the accident? They were speeding. Fast as lightning. They'd crossed into the opposite lane, gone over the hard shoulder, and plowed into the trunk of a plane tree. The *S*'s ended before the asphalt did. The brother who was driving had taken his foot off the brake pedal.

Why had he released the brake? Why hadn't he held out until the final moment? Had he given up? Had he understood that there was nothing he could do? Not even soften the blow, no matter how slightly? Or was it that, when there is nothing to be done, the body relaxes and accepts its fate? Or did the driver want to escape the car? Did he want to get out in that half of a second? Half a second? What is a half second? But did he try anyway? You have to do something with the time, no matter how little there is, something to fill that desperate wait, a moment like that, and perhaps his body focused on that rift; did his whole being shrink painfully to get through it and leap out of the car in half a second? The driver didn't know what half a second was. He had no idea. No one does. No one knows what half a second is. Life is made up of half seconds. Life is half a second. But it turned out that he had no idea. How long would it last? Did he have time? Perhaps he wasn't wearing his seat belt. What luck! In the panic, the idea traveled at the speed of light. It became porous and ramified his brain. His blood became adrenaline. Dynamite. It flooded that half second, or what was left of that half second, the longest half second of his life: half a second of explosions, half a second that the driver would have lengthened or shortened infinitely, but was only able to turn into the best utilized half second, the most lived half second of his life. A terrorific farewell, the skull awaiting the bullet, a half second that never reaches its end but will be over at any moment—when you least expect it, suddenly, but what do you do in the meantime? How do you spend it? The more you concentrate on it, the longer it becomes. And you're waiting for it, you can't stop waiting for it! Half a second of perverse, labyrinthine corners, of torture chambers, vaults, and monstrous self-discoveries, of mirrors and windows, of holes that lead to stairs, half a second filled with alarms that rush you, with the loves you forgot until now, with friends who've come to say good-bye, waiting, lined up on the branches of the plane tree. Half a second filled with ideas, with joys and unexpected comforts, with solutions: for example suicide, but he doesn't have time to beat death, he won't even have time to escape or accept it, even though he leaves his mark on the asphalt, an oscillogram of the last seconds, a final signature. He heard the sound of his braking run through the fields to Vidreres to warn everyone, and smelled the burning rubber, and that brother who was driving thought of his parents, cursing the disgrace and grief he was leaving behind—their lands, their lands, how would they get along without him?— he felt filled with rage for that which he could not prevent, for not being able to control the situation, for still being alive and not being able to do anything, and suddenly he remembered his brother.

He was right beside him. He was with him. His hair stood on end when he grasped that. His brother with eyes wide as saucers, scared out of his wits just like him, and he suddenly realized that it was all over. His brother trusted him—he had no choice—but he couldn't give him the steering wheel, and he thought: Now how do I let him know there's nothing to be done, when my body is so slow that I don't even have time to open my mouth. I only have half a second! How do I tell him that I want to leap out of the car and leave him alone here, that I've lost control, that it's my fault, this accident, that I'm the one who will plow us into the tree? How do I confess to him that I've taken my foot off the pedal and if I can, I'll abandon him without even saying good-bye?

The car, flying toward the tree's trunk.

Ernest took his foot off the accelerator.

Two days earlier, on the morning of the accident, he was many kilometers from there, at home, sleeping with his wife, in a room that shared a wall with his eldest daughter's bedroom.

There was a bouquet of flowers tied to the trunk. He would have liked to stop and have a calm look around. He would have liked to keep thinking about the deaths, searching for signs of the dead boys scattered amid the bits of glass and plastic around the trunk. He had made a discovery: thinking about them calmed him down. His thoughts were alive, impossible to kill. He would die before his thoughts. The boys, in his head, were immortal. Perhaps he should tell their parents. A stranger was protecting their sons.

But he didn't stop when he saw the plane tree. They had beat him to it. A couple of teenagers were looking at the bouquet from their motorcycles, stopped on the side of the highway with their mudguards pointing toward the tree.

He continued slowly, driving more through the landscape than along the highway, as if he wanted to save himself from the accident, as if he was now accompanying the two brothers and passing by death, taking them—sitting in his back seat—along a highway of embers, unable to stop, open to the landscape just like every day as he went from his house to the office and from the office to his house, his favorite times, in the summer because it was summer and in the winter because it was winter, but today with an intensity that surpassed him: saving himself, leaving the plain behind. He was fleeing. He was finishing off the two boys. They were no longer there. He had taken part in the brothers' deaths. He had designed and poured the highway's asphalt; he planted the tree. He was guilty of two deaths, his guilt made it all make sense, so he could escape from it, because it was all programmed, it headed toward his own salvation. Farewell, see you never. He sacrificed the two boys for his family.

He was already stepping on the gas when he heard the motorcycles behind him. He saw them in the rearview mirror, and slowed up again to wait for the teenagers to pass him. When they were out of sight he exited the highway at the first road he came across, turned around, and went back to the scene of the accident.

He swerved his Megane onto the shoulder. He parked where the motorcycles had stopped before and found it all banal: the black *S*'s on the asphalt, the bouquet of flowers tied with a white ribbon around the wounded tree trunk, and the smattering of glass on the ground. The violence of the accident—the extinction of two lives—had nothing in common with the stillness of the tree nor with the cement mass of the Montseny in the background. He remembered the car in the photograph with its engine on the ground, the mourners, the parents' sobs. They had nothing to do with it either.

The highway that linked Vidreres with the main freeway had little traffic. He heard the rhythm of some music a kilometer away. He looked up. The girl from before was dancing, holding her cell phone to her ear. It was just a moment, the music rode in on a gust of wind. He could no longer hear it, but he was captivated by the sight of the girl's hair and white dress, silhouetted against the fields and little houses of Vidreres. The distance made her dancing more precise. The flame of a candle in memory of the boys. Suddenly, the girl was still. A truck was approaching. It was the truck that was loaded down with hay before. Its turn signal flashed and it slowed. The girl got excited and took up her dance again, more joyfully, to convince the client, or maybe to show him that she wasn't dancing for him.

The truck left the highway onto the access road, and stopped just past the girl. The driver stuck his head out of the window and looked back without turning off the engine or his turn signal. Ernest recognized him. The girl continued dancing. The truck driver started waving to get her attention. He must have been shouting at her. The girl danced as if she didn't hear him, with her cell phone against her ear. The driver disappeared back into the cab of his truck. He shut off the engine. He got out and stood by the door, hands on his hips. The girl didn't even look at him. The driver put a hand in his pocket, pulled out his wallet, opened it, and held out a bill to her. He waved it at her. The girl stopped. The trucker put the bill back in his wallet. The girl walked toward him. Then he leaped into the cab and started the engine. When she reached the driver's side door, the truck's horn blared with such violence that the girl jumped onto the highway without looking. If a car had been passing just then, she would have been hit.

The truck backed up a few meters. The girl followed it. The truck accelerated. Finally, the girl stopped. The truck stopped too. The girl again walked toward the truck. When she was beneath the driver's side window, he honked the horn again. The girl covered her ears. She turned to leave. Then the trucker stuck his arm out of the window and closed his hand, leaving his middle finger raised. The girl turned, made the same gesture, and started to shout, but over the noise of the truck she couldn't be heard.

The truck driver advanced slowly until he reached Ernest's car. He stopped the truck behind it and got out.

"What a whore," he said. "Did you see that? When I showed her the bill it got her attention . . . fucking whore. Maybe she thought I'd pay her a hundred euros! Who knows what she's on. Look how she's dancing."

She had turned to dance facing them, to provoke them. The truck driver lifted his arm.

"Little whore! . . . Littttle whooore! . . . Come here, you little pussy! . . . There are two of us! Litttle whooore! . . . Come here, littttle whooore!"

The girl made another rude gesture, turned her back to him, and kept dancing.

"When they're high they don't concentrate," said the truck driver. "But I have to admit she's really hot. You gotta admit she's really hot. Thin with small breasts, easy handling . . . A little ass the size of my hands. An easy little pussy. There aren't many like that. You see, over on the other side of the highway?"

There was a white van half-hidden behind a tree.

"She's new. They're keeping an eye on her. I'm not surprised, she's out of this world that whore—I could lose my mind over her. Am I right or am I right? What do you say? Sure is a coincidence to find such a nice piece, just the way I like 'em, isn't it? Let's see. How can it be that I'd find her here, on this bit of lost highway, right as I'm passing by, when I never go this way? A new girl? Was she waiting for me? Right now if somebody said: Tell me, Miqui, what kind of girl are you looking for exactly? Ask for whatever you want. How do you want her? Like this one, yes or no? Would you change anything about her? No. Could you improve her? Impossible. Well, here you go. All for you. Seriously, man, wouldn't you be suspicious? Really, I don't know. Maybe I shouldn't be suspicious. But I'm cranky. I've had a crappy morning. Maybe it's instinct. A man can get it on with a goat, with a hen, with another guy, if need be. I don't know, maybe she's not as hot as she looks, you know what I mean? What do you say? What do you think? Look at her. Is she fine or what?"

"Too young."

"She's super hot. It's so obvious. What, you like old ones, or what? The problem is she's high. When they're high they don't concentrate."

Then the truck driver saw the bouquet of flowers on the tree.

"Shit," he said. "They must be fresh, too."

"I didn't know them," said Ernest, as if he'd been caught

taking advantage of a tragedy. "I don't know anything about it. I work in Vidreres, but I'm not from here."

"Well, it's lucky not to be from here today. Unless you've got my bad luck, because I had to deliver some bales of hay to the house of the girlfriend of one of the guys who died at this tree. There were two of them. This was their final stop. I had to spend the morning in the social club's bar, scratching my ass with the girl who works there, and then her dad told me they just came from the burial of a very close friend of their daughter's. Then I saw the daughter . . . oh man."

A few cars passed, coming from town. The drivers slowed down and glanced at the tree.

"We're idiots," said the trucker. He walked past the plane tree and pissed behind the trunk. "We should be used to it by now. You think thirty or forty years will make a difference? Even fifty, you think that'll make a lick of difference?"

"The years don't belong to you, no."

"They never belong to you," said the truck driver.

"When I got here, there were some kids," he said in his defense.

The trucker came around the plane tree, zipping up his fly. He stepped on the broken glass, extended his hand, and pulled a flower out of the bouquet.

"We must be taking turns. First the kids, then you, then me . . . " he said. "Do you know Cindy?"

"Cindy from the club?"

"She is a fox, too, isn't she?" He plucked another flower and turned. "I don't get it. Why do people put out flowers? It's bullshit. Where do you usually die? At home or in the hospital, right? And no one puts out flowers there.

These bunches of flowers bug me. Dead people don't give a shit about flowers. You take flowers to the cemetery, not the highway. Two days from now nobody's even going to remember. It's disgusting, rotting flowers all over; I see them everywhere. We should be happy, shit, two more chicks for us; let's worry about the girls. Damn, that one over there was nothing to sneeze at. She was begging for some tenderness."

Ernest went toward the car. Sometimes it seemed that men chose him. Even old ones, they looked back and said to him: Ah, when I was young! Ah, if I were young again! At the bank he was used to guys bragging about money, clients who puffed up their chests and looked at him arrogantly—he spends his days touching other people's money, poor loser!—without imagining that in the very chair where they were then sitting, still warm, the last client had moved fifty or a hundred times more money than those braggarts, money that these show-offs couldn't even imagine was flowing through Vidreres. But sexual vanity had an arrogance and a defiance to it that vanity over wealth didn't. You can't live without money, but you can live without sex, so these sexual creatures boast about something more gratuitous, more pure and free. And if it's just their nature, then it's even worse to brag. There was nothing to brag about then. They want to get you mixed up in their lies. He gave thanks for the success of his marriage, for the modesty of his desires, for the unequal distribution of things: how nature makes skinny gluttons and fat ascetics, and he was one of the former. He had always been like that, it wasn't a question of age.

The trucker pointed with the flowers to a dent in the truck's fender.

"I would have made mincemeat of that tree," he said. "Get into the cab for a minute, come on, you'll see how different it is than a car."

He said no, but accepted a cigarette. He saw that the girl had left. He hadn't smoked since his second daughter was born. Twenty years. Now, the sting made him feel the outline of his tongue, the walls of his mouth. He wanted to think it was his family and friends who helped him to be himself, but the two dead boys, the unhinged truck driver, the very taste of the tobacco was helping him much more. Otherwise, what were they doing there? What made him stop there? Now, after a delay, he thought he understood what had happened. Before the truck driver showed up he had the impression of his life being captured within walls of the dead, of feeling compressed by the death around him, the dead turning into his skin, his shape, his protection against a chaotic and ephemeral world; the cadavers converted into the only breakwater against the waves of time. The dead gave life shape: everything outside of Ernest was dead, the dead were dead, but the tree was also dead, and the truck driver was dead, and the prostitute was dead too. That was why he felt so bad and so alone, but also why he had to endure. If he went home and found his daughters and wife dead, he wouldn't have lost an arm, or a lung: he would keep breathing, keep going to work at the bank every day. He would still be whole, even more whole then, with more experience. Ernest had a potbelly but was in good health. Why worry about the dent in the fender the trucker was pointing at? Why worry about the deaths of people he'd never met? Was suffering necessary? Or did he enjoy it?

The trucker was right. We are idiots. How embarrassingly gratuitous suffering is, how contemptible. Keeping everyone who was dying at that moment present was an insult to the luck of not being in their skin. He didn't suffer for the dead boys; he didn't suffer for his daughters. He suffered for himself, for his cowardice, and he was eaten up by shame.

"What's the dent from?" he asked.

"I don't know. A couple of months ago I made a trip to Breda with construction materials. Because now you never know where you'll get sent, any day I'll have to go to Belgium or the ends of the earth, and that's if I'm lucky. The fucking construction bust, it's worse than they say, it's all illegal trucks now, everybody's a trucker now that there's nothing to transport. So I had to go to Breda. It was already dark on the way back, I felt a jolt, but I didn't stop. If it was a dog or a boar, it was dead. I glanced in the mirror and didn't see anything on the road. Anyway, when an animal crosses the highway, the last thing you should do is try to dodge it, unless you want to have an accident. I don't know what it was, maybe a ball. It wouldn't have been the first time I've had an animal stuck to the fender, but when I got home there was nothing there. I know a trucker who once brought back a roe deer from the Pyrenees. He didn't find it until the next day. He saw a stain on the ground, he thought his truck was losing oil, but it was a roe deer that was still breathing."

The trucker climbed into the cab, put the flowers on the dashboard, lowered the window, and said, "Hop on in, you'll see."

"I've gotta go."

"Look," said the truck driver. "You can leave with a clear conscience. They're coming to relieve us."

At first he didn't recognize him. Then he saw that it was Mr. Cals. He was walking with a cane that he'd never seen before. He looked mechanical, black and robust like a spider.

"You came to see the tree too?" said Mr. Cals.

He felt like a tourist at a concentration camp. Mr. Cals must have more reasons for being there. He lifted his cane and aimed it at a point amid the fields, with the mountains of the Ardenya in the background.

"Every day after lunch I stretch my legs, walking all the way to Clar stream," he said. "You won't find a flatter plain anywhere... take a good look. Those trees over there are Puig's forest. That's Cal Borni. There, Can Batllosera. Do you see anything special?"

This eighty-year-old spider is voracious, thought Ernest, he's very experienced, he rams in his chelicerae, waits for the poison to hit the insect he's hunted, and then he eats it.

"The lands of Can Batlle," said Ernest.

"Can Batlle is on the other side of town. No. These fields... You see how flat they are? In 1937, during the war, they made an airfield here. Workers started to come, mostly from Sant Feliu, three hundred men showed up. Vidreres, in those days, was no more than two thousand, and that's counting the two hundred war refugees from Madrid who'd already arrived. The clouds of dust they raised, moving all the earth, the tractors... They still filled the trucks with shovels! They changed the course of Rere Pins and Can Canyet's irrigation channel, they buried storehouses for bombs and gas tanks...and in '38, in March, it must have been about six, because we were coming out of school, we saw planes with four wings coming in from the west, and they landed, and they were still running along the strip when Ballartet, who was a kid like me, Ballartet lifted his finger to the sky, and we saw a silvery dot, like a needle. It was an observation plane—the kind we called *Pava*—from Franco's forces, with three escort planes. The excitement didn't last long. Within four days the first bombing began. Three planes at nine in the morning. A bomb fell where Can Met is now. Antoni Amargant and Pep from Casa Nova, who are dead now, were going to the village on bicycles, and when they heard the planes they threw themselves to the ground. And Pep was on the side closest to the road, and the shrapnel hit him and he lost an arm. Spent the rest of his life in Vidreres with one empty sleeve. Bombs fell where Can Rafel is now, breaking all the windowpanes, and on one of Torre's fields, on Modeguet and Can Castelló; it's a miracle they didn't kill Encarna Mauri. It was a bad spot for an airfield, one of those ideas the Republic had, putting a field here just because it was flat. The National forces came from Majorca, and when they passed Mont Barbat they were right over us... There was no time to do anything: when you heard the roar of the engines the bombs had already started. Five days later, a couple more planes attacked us. I remember that it hadn't rained in a long time, and the earth was so dry that the bombs sent chunks flying higher than the tops of the pine and cork trees, so much dust, and a bomb fell on the woodshed of Can Súria, everybody was in the shelter except for Genové and Miquel Vives from Sils, who were working in the field, and both got killed." Mr. Cals grabbed Ernest by the arm. "First thing the next morning they attacked the field again, because it was April 14, the anniversary of the Republic. I was headed to school. I saw the middle of the field all lit up... and the planes ran along the strip so they wouldn't get hit—the lights were bombs... Ambulances ran all morning. They blew up the gas tank at the Campsa, they killed three pilots and a lieutenant, four dead..."

"I have to go for lunch," shouted the trucker from his cab, starting the engine. "Come along. Trust me!"

"You know where there was a shelter, during the war?" continued Mr. Cals. "Right in front of your bank, in the church square... When they dug it they found human bones, that always happens when you poke around near a church... We went in there to play, I remember it as if it were yesterday."

"Follow me!" shouted the trucker from his cab.

He left Mr. Cals there, obviously still wanting to reminisce, and headed to his car.

He followed the truck to get away from Mr. Cals. He was headed away from his house, but before he could make up his mind to turn around, the truck pulled into the parking lot of a restaurant on the side of the highway.

The chalkboard advertised a nine-euro prix fixe menu. He parked. He called home so they wouldn't expect him for lunch. Some unexpected work had come up at the office. He was staying with Jaume to go over some accounts that didn't add up. He got out of the car and entered the restaurant with the trucker. At the very back was a lit fireplace. Most of the customers were truck drivers. They were talking from one table to the next, shouting because they'd been drinking and had time—the tachometer was in charge, they had to take their required hours of rest. But the shouting could also have been from excitement, from truckers who had no time to waste.

"I don't know what I'm doing," he said out loud.

"Order the lamb and you'll know. This is definitely better than standing there staring at some bullshit tree. You work this afternoon? I'm done for the day. I sometimes have days with nothing to do. Tomorrow I have to go pick up a boat, next Monday I go to Vic to load up some scrap metal, after that we'll see. I'll give you my card, you never know."

Was there sexual tension coming from the trucker, or from him? He lowered his gaze, saw his potbelly, and decided there wasn't.

"I work mornings."

"What are you, a civil servant?"

"I work at the Santander Bank in Vidreres."

The other man took a step back.

"Don't tell me I'm having lunch with a banker."

"A commercial manager, an employee at a bank… I wouldn't call myself a banker."

"I've got a problem with bankers. Particularly one in my town, in Sils. You stiffed my dad out of his money. You screwed him over, which means screwing me over too. When I see a Mercedes I know it's a banker, or a politician, or both. One of these days I'm going lose my cool, grab a shotgun, get into my cab, and start taking justice into my own hands."

"Go right ahead, as far as I'm concerned."

"Don't say that twice. Look out the window. See that kid? They come around with demijohns, force open the gas caps, stick a hose in there, suck a little, and that's all she wrote. My gas tank holds three hundred liters. You do the math. I have to go around at almost empty all the time. One of these days I'm gonna get stuck halfway to somewhere. A few weeks ago they showed up with a van that had a three thousand-liter reservoir. A plastic reservoir inside the van with a pumping system to steal diesel from the trucks. One of those trailers has a thousand-liter tank. You do the math. But if they catch them at it, then what? They won't do any time. They're forgiving of thieves, you know, wolves don't bite other wolves. And at least you can see them. The problem with you bankers is we don't see you do it."

He was the spider himself. He ate the lamb while thinking about the brothers. The boy from outside was the same age as the two dead ones; he had come into the restaurant and was sitting at the bar.

Ernest left half of his meal. He felt like he was outside the world, reduced like a plant to the most basic functions: breathing, eating.

The waitress served them dessert and said, laughing, "Miqui, say 'hi' to Cloe for me!"

"How did she know?" said Miqui, when she had left. "What a bitch . . . You know how she knows I'm going to see her? Because I didn't order the garlic mayonnaise."

Wherever they were and in whatever state, the last thing the two brothers would be thinking about, if they were able to think about anything at all, would be coming back. Yet these two men, his wife, his three daughters, Mr. Cals, all

the customers in that restaurant, the survivors of the bomb-
ings, these survivors of Saturday's accident, had all thought at
some point about how to stay here, how to escape death, their
own death and the deaths of their loved ones, which is the
same thing. Escape from it like the brother wanting to leap
out of the car at the last minute. But, while the dead knew
where to return to and chose not to, the living didn't know
where to go to escape. And they all had fantasies like he did:
they imagined strategies, switching places with someone else,
leaping from one living body to another like hopping from
one rock to the next so as not to fall into the river. That's what
he should have done, rather than having three daughters who
chained him to this world. Any of those diners, Miqui himself... maybe that's why he had followed him, maybe that's
why he was here. You take my car, I'll take your truck, each
of us will escape our death; we'll speed off in opposite direc-
tions, we'll take on the other's destruction and not our own.

"What happened to the fender?"

"Nothing."

"Why did you show it to me?"

"I didn't show you anything. Maybe I didn't do it, that
dent; maybe it was my father before he gave me the truck,
in that accident. He just went off the highway, the next day
a tow truck came and pulled the truck out, it was nothing,
but he'd had enough, it shook him up. That evening he had
a heart attack. We didn't notice a thing; the doctor told us
after my dad was dragging himself around like a zombie for
weeks. In the meantime, a perfect opportunity for the bank
to rip him off."

How could he explain what he was doing to his wife and

daughters? Wasn't it running away? Can you escape without betrayal? Can you escape?

"Fucking heartless bankers. How can you not have noticed Cindy?" said Miqui. "That's a wedding ring you're wearing, right? Do you have any idea why I've had such a hard time staying with any one woman? I must've had bad luck. Maybe I needed something special. Like a South American chick. That one's a total fox. A little short, but grade A stuff. Cindy. Just her name gets your motor running. I'm a good catch . . . well . . . I'm a good catch for her. Where's she from? Bolivia? Paraguay? Exotic, half Indian, with that accent that . . . She talks like us, but she came from the other side of the world. Who knows why. That's the problem with chicks. You think two guys could ever be as different as a guy and a girl are?"

"Look at us."

"What's wrong? I forgive you for being a banker."

"Don't count on ever seeing me again."

"Does she have a boyfriend, Cindy?"

"Cindy is a child."

"She's a fox."

"Leave her alone."

"Shit. You bankers think you own the world, huh? You're like civil servants, living like kings at the expense of poor stooges like me and my dad. I bet you have kids. Fuck, I guess you guys have to fill your time somehow. And that potbelly. And that jacket. And deciding who gets close to Cindy and who doesn't. Unbelievable. What's wrong, you saw her first or something? My ass. You didn't even notice her. You have to know how to see girls. It's not as easy as it looks. It's something you learn. Now that I've spotted her, she's got you all hot under the collar. Your wife not enough for you, huh? You've got some balls. I feel sorry for you, I have to admit. If I were you, I might do the same thing. When I leave here I'm going to see some girlfriends. You wanna come with me?"

"I can just imagine your girlfriends."

"What's wrong with my friends?"

"No, thanks."

"You haven't seen them. Don't be in such a rush. You aren't made of stone. Look how worked up you got over a little spic piece of ass. They've got us by the balls, that's what I always say. They should teach it at school. Strategies for resisting them. Just like you learn not to piss the bed. They should've prepared us when we were little."

"Those girls are kidnapped from their countries. Everyone knows that. They drug them, they beat and rape them, they kidnap them, they threaten to kill their families. They're found dead on the side of the road and they can't be identified, nobody knows anything about them. They find them destroyed, twenty-year-old girls, on this highway right here."

"And if you screw them your dick falls off. You've seen too many movies. I'm telling you, none of that is true. It's not against the law."

"Because we pretend they don't exist."

"Well, if they do exist, I guess they have to eat. It's a business like any other; life is rough for everyone, except the bankers. Don't look at me like that. I'm a good guy. I've never left without paying. I've never hit any of them. Now you're gonna say that other businesses are different. And that, coming from a banker, for fuck's sake."

"Let's forget about it. But I'd prefer not to see you in Vidreres again."

"Now you're the sheriff again. When I've got my shotgun, you want me to lend it to you, or what? You've got some balls. You're threatening me, right? You're threatening me, right, banker? A fucking coward, threatening me? What the hell were you doing there at the tree? Do you talk to the dead or what? Didn't you say you didn't know them? That's spineless. You think about them to avoid thinking about your own fucking life. I know a few guys like you. Starting with my father, or that old guy by the tree. There was a war, poor him! When he was a kid! And he's still not over it! Shit, what a good deal. Eighty, ninety years later and he's still thinking about it. My mother died when I was this tall. You see me crying? Do you? No, we won't forget about it. Come with me to see the girls. Grow a pair, man. It's all very well that you want to have balls, banker, but you can't just talk. Come on, shake a leg. You'll be a big hit in that suit. Let's go see them. Right after lunch is a good time. You'll see, all your hang-ups will disappear, just like that."

III

He saw the tree again, the bouquet of flowers, the ribbon snake bandaging the wound. He drove, following the truck: they were headed to Lloret. Before they got there they left the highway and entered a housing development, passing over empty streets named after flowers. The street where they stopped only had one sidewalk, with detached houses. To build the houses they had emptied out the granite, which still showed its teeth between some of them. There were houses with swimming-pool blue awnings, rolled up and faded, lethargic summer homes with lawns hibernating in front. A single car parked on the entire street, no smoke from any chimney—little hills filled with empty houses. The trucker got out of his cab with the flowers in his hand.

"You thought I was gonna take you to some club, banker?"

When he had to make a big decision—approving a mortgage, giving a credit line for a risky business operation—the bank employee thought about his daughters. Normally he decided in their favor, but sometimes he decided against them. The trucker rang the doorbell. They heard a girl's voice.

"Just a minute!"

The door opened and it was a blonde, like a projection from youth. Healthy face, precise movements. The trucker held a flower out to her.

"Miqui ... how sweet! Marga!" she turned into the house. "They're here!"

This was Cloe, the one the waitress had mentioned. They kissed on each cheek, and then the two men followed her through the hallway toward the empty dining room.

"Would you like some coffee? Marga! Marga!"

Marga had just taken a shower. She was wearing a tight, matching blue outfit with a short skirt like her friend's. Nothing like the girls on the highway. She and Miqui gave each other kisses on each cheek, and Marga received the second flower.

They couldn't have gone out onto the street dressed like that. Ernest tried to figure out which girl was for the trucker and which one was for him. It wasn't like on the highway, where you just passed them by. Perhaps it was sordid, just a few hours after the burial, perhaps the trucker was sordid, perhaps the housing development was ... but the girls' skin made the sordidness seem far, far away. He couldn't decide between them, and he was afraid that, if the trucker discovered which one he wanted, he would take her from him. His body made the decision all on its own, choosing Marga, with her hair still damp from the shower and combed back, with all the skin on her face revealed as a pale mask against the bright color of her earrings, which hung like stone worms from her earlobes. He had never had a girl like this so close to him before. His daughters couldn't hold a candle to her. There was no shelter from the carnal bombing.

"How ya doing, Miqui?" said Marga.

"You two are my downfall."

The girl must have gotten cold, because she put on a short, tight red leather jacket and sat beside Ernest, with the tips of her hair dripping onto her leather shoulders. She had the flower on her knees, held in one hand. She put it on the table, with the other. He touched her leg with his pants. He felt stuck to her, threaded through her earrings, overlapped like half of the zipper, stuck together by the pull whose paint was peeled, which meant she'd worn the jacket more than it seemed, so bright and waxy, so new-seeming with the damp hair. The girl's long fingers had gripped the pull a thousand times to open and close the jacket. It hadn't been long since that jacket had been in contact with her adolescence.

"That's why I brought my banker friend," said Miqui, winking and gesturing to say: choose the one you want. "We met... Have you ever done it with a guy from South America?"

"Don't be weird," said Cloe.

"I met a chick from somewhere down there."

"You never stop," said the girl.

"You have no idea. Times are bad now, but remember Ahmed? The Arab guy who used to come with me in the truck—I don't need him now, there's no work, but I'm talking about the good times, five or six years ago. One Saturday we left Vallcanera in the morning with the truck, and we did the whole highway. We left no stone unturned. When we got to La Jonquera that night, shit, we dropped dead at the Paradise. Four in the morning, both of us, first him then me—we switched off, and took whatever chick we got. Shit. It was like we were high as kites but we hadn't taken a thing, we were laughing so hard we almost pissed our pants. We ate in Banyoles, took a snooze by the lake on the grass, and kept going up toward the border. To see who would cry uncle first. You know, the further north you go, the more material. The whore would climb into the cab, and one of us would go take a piss—you didn't come back until the other whistled. We kept our eyes on the prize, and whatever you got you had to make do with; if you got an old cow, tough luck. We held up like sons of guns. We were in a dead heat. I could do a porn film, I swear. Isn't that right? The next day, we kept going, back down from the border, wanting to break the tie, first him then me and on and on like that. But there was no way. We exited at Banyoles again for a rest and got to Sils that night, destroyed, still laughing our asses off. And we weren't drunk, but we couldn't stop laughing and shouting like lunatics, fucking hell, Ahmed, and with the music blaring. We didn't need to drink; we had central heating! Those whores couldn't finish us off in one week-end, no way! We were wrecked! Fucking Ahmed! Wonder where he is now. Must have gone back to Morocco, fucking hell. I wouldn't do that again for anything in the world, banker."

One of the girls had gone to the kitchen to get some beer. The walls in the house were too clean, the paint couldn't have been more than six months old, but the dining room looked lived in. The few furnishings were cheap but new.

He could still feel the kisses on his face, the fresh saliva, warm and corrosive like the exfoliating creams housewives use to get their skin shiny and clean, the water of the fountain of youth in a painting he had seen on the cover of a magazine at the bank, men and women bathing in rejuvenating waters . . . And, at the same time, how exhausting . . . man wasn't the result of evolution from animals, man was already there: there was no evolution, only taming, vigilance—but the hierarchy was still fresh . . . Man drinks and eats, copulates and urinates, breathes and sleeps and looks at his cage as if it were a mirror, fascinated, suspicious, imprisoned as well. How can he hope to return home, that man in the zoo looking at the animals? On which side of the bars is his house? And all the years of watching over the animal were exhausting, the way he's exhausted by the temptation to leap to the other side, to avail himself of his rights . . . . He couldn't lose his freedom, accept that there's a boss without creating a scene, accept it like the girls accepted them: a sweaty trucker flecked with straw, a potbellied office worker stinking of garlic mayonnaise . . .

"Hey, what are you thinking about? You're on some other planet!" shouted Cloe. "What's wrong with this guy?" And she laughed and started kissing Miqui. "Come on, man, you're gonna have fun!"

He couldn't imagine hugging Marga with the other two there. He had to wash himself, get the animal off him. But he shouldn't wash all of it off either.

He glanced at Marga, ashamed, with the same shame that animals have—the way they lower their gaze and their ears when they're around humans.

His contemplation was already an access into her, and

maybe what he had to do was be satisfied with that, just get up and leave.

"There's plenty of fish in the sea," his father told him the first time he broke up with a girl.

There were plenty of fish and no: he would never understand what they had in common, what made them women, what made them different from him.

"Hello? Hello? Helllllooo?..."

The other two were nibbling on each other like they were in love, and he couldn't even speak. She would eventually react, that was her job. Had he become so unappealing over the years? Didn't his body have the right to get close to these bodies? Or was that precisely what would make the act more human?

"Hello? Hello? Don't you like me? These handsome office workers... you have so much time to think..."

It wasn't having time that made him think, but having relations. And he would think about this for quite some time. It had happened once with a client. She and her husband owned the Vidreres hardware store. Twice a week she came by the office to make a deposit. She was older than him— that was before Ernest had a potbelly. They agreed to meet after work, saying they had some details to discuss about a pension plan. They were so discreet about their intentions that they met at the social club right across from the office. Cindy didn't work there then. The waiter made the rounds of the tables. Ernest wrote a few numbers on a piece of paper on the marble tabletop, and, among the figures, without looking up: "I like you." And then he added, in a trembling hand: "A lot." And then, in all caps: "A LOT." And once more, the pen going through the paper: "A WHOLE LOT." He wanted to write: "I'm shocked by this, I can't believe it, what am I doing?" He wanted to keep writing what he was feeling, revealing it and revealing himself to her. Was he himself? And she, was she? "I'll wait for you on the corner," he wrote, and made a diagram with an arrow pointing to a car. "Blue Megane." The same one he still had.

He drove with one eye on the mirror, afraid he was being followed, and veered into the forest. The next day she called the office, and he hung up without saying anything.

You aren't the one who decides . . . the girls don't decide to be on the highway, the boys didn't decide to kill themselves, the trucker's father hadn't decided to be scammed, he hadn't decided to come here. The girls were too young. No man could resist them.

This was nothing like the highway. These girls earned more than his two eldest daughters put together. The little one spent all day at home, online. Of course, he thought. My daughters should take this business up. I mean it, girls. From the bottom of my heart.

"I'll bring you another beer," said Marga, getting up.

Thinking wasn't a question of time, but rather a question of space, of intensity. You could think about two contradictory things without any contradiction, in closed compartments, because the brain worked in layers. There's a party going on upstairs; on the floor below, someone is trying to sleep. You hear the music from the party, and those up there know that every stomp, every dance step, will be heard down below. Regrets above and headaches below, but each private, without being communicated. Most of the time, the brain isn't a two-story house, but a skyscraper forty or two hundred floors tall, with a different landscape out each window. If it were just one floor, it wouldn't matter which one. Being forced to live on more than one simultaneously gets you used to relativism. You have forty, two hundred thousand lives. But, on the other hand, you have to choose, because you have to be someone, you have to be a role model for your daughters, at least, for the people you love, you don't want to be an example of solitude, you don't want to leave them alone, you want them to know that you are here, in one window or another. You aren't an irresponsible cad. And so what does he decide? To take advantage of the fact that the girl is in the kitchen to stand up and flee? What is going with the flow? Staying or leaving? What does he want? Shouldn't he know that? Otherwise, what's he doing here? How could he not know? Doesn't he know if he wants it? Isn't indecision a worse sin? If you're going to make a mistake, at least save yourself the suffering! If only you could leap! From the twenty-first floor! From the car speeding toward the tree!

He suddenly remembered something one of his cousins once told him at the tail end of a wedding reception, when the dancing had begun and there were only three people left at their table: his cousin, a bearded man, and him. The bride passed near them, and the bearded guy made some comment about her ass. His cousin's face changed suddenly, and he told him he could cut out the crassness.

"That kind of comment," he said, looking into the eyes of the bearded man, who was at least as drunk as he was, "always comes from guys who aren't getting any, guys who resent women."

The bearded man was slow to grasp what he'd just been told, but then he answered with the same rudeness he'd used to describe the girl's ass—and which made his cousin realize that the comment wasn't coming from carefree joie de vivre, but was tinged with self-indulgence and in bad faith—and, still smiling: "There's no merit in getting some if you have to pay for it."

"No one's talking about merit here," answered the cousin. And then he said the words that haunted Ernest for weeks, to the point that it changed the frequency of his sexual relations with his wife. His cousin said: "I look for a bit of life without hurting anyone. That's why I pay for it, but I don't recommend it to others."

The girl came back with more beers.

"What?" she said, taking his hand.

She didn't know how to take an old man's hand; she took it in hers carefully, like a teenager, and tried to tug. He pulled it away. He emptied his beer in three gulps. A happy feeling of release washed over him. As he waited for her to finish her beer, he saw the other girl's hair at his friend's waist.

"Let's go to a room," he said.

Learn to live for once. For once, learn to think about your family from many floors up or down, move away from the windows, learn to live without them for the day you'll have to leave, for the day they leave.

In the girl's room there were towels from the shower and scattered clothes. Some pants, a skirt, and a blouse. The furniture in there was new too, and there was nothing hanging on the walls. They didn't live here. But the door to the closet was half open, revealing colorful dresses and shoes.

The girl drew the curtains and turned off the light. The room was left quite dark. He took off his clothes, imitating her. He got into the bed. He was embarrassed by his body. The age difference was obscene, and he would have preferred she approach him dressed, because he also desired her clothes. She wore a purple lingerie set. She had a tattoo at the base of her neck, ivy that went down the middle of her back.

"Are you okay?" she asked.

"Close the door. Don't talk."

"All right, but close your eyes."

Ernest closed his eyes and waited. The bed started to warm up, the sheets were clean; no one had slept there.

He heard the trucker laugh on the other side of the door. What was taking her so long? Was she going to get into bed with him or pull the covers off him?

Women don't know their power, nor how to depersonalize that power. The less they are like themselves, the stronger they are. The girl moved around the room, but he resisted opening his eyes until he remembered that he had left his wallet in his pants, with his ID and four fifty-euro bills.

He opened his eyes. He saw some sort of angel in front of the wardrobe. He closed his eyes and opened them again. The girl smiled in the half-light. She was wearing the purple lingerie set, the earrings, and some white wings with plastic feathers.

He had seen those wings in Vidreres, in the window of the sex shop, and now he understood why there was a sex shop in a small, rural town like Vidreres: for prostitutes and their clients.

It seemed like everything was becoming clear.

"Tell me one thing," he said. "What did you do this morning?"

The girl didn't answer. She knew the two boys. She was in the square, she was at the church, she had accompanied them to the cemetery.

"Answer me."

"You told me not to talk."

The wings were as violent and awkward as plowshares. The girl knew the two dead boys. Both girls knew them. How could they not? They were the same age. Everyone had gone to the funeral.

"Where were you earlier today?"

The girl no longer laughed.

"What do you care?"

He got up from the bed. His daughters had grown up, and he'd had to learn not to raise his hand to them. But there were moments when you had to. When you have children you spend your life risking your dignity. Your existence lies in the hands of someone else. That's what children are. They destroy you. There should be some way to retire after having them. Retire from being a parent. Since there isn't, you have to stay in shape to deal with them. Deal with your children; deal with the young. The girl could have been his daughter. And just as he would have with his daughters, he got up from the bed and planted himself in front of her. One more rude remark and he'd slap her.

"Get back in bed," she said. She had lowered her gaze. "Get back in bed, will you? Close your eyes again . . . try to relax . . . We were out—in the winter this place is dead—we were in Barcelona earlier, at a gym, if you really want to know. Okay? Do you mind? What's wrong with you? This was a special surprise for you."

She meant the wings. Ernest got back in bed and closed his eyes. The girl lay down beside him. She kissed him on the cheek like a daughter, until he turned toward her and opened his eyes and hugged her and stroked her. She had taken off the wings but still wore the lingerie set, and she was smiling again. Innocent as animals, he thought. They live in Barcelona, they come up here to work, and then they go back. It's a parenthesis. An upper floor. They are named Clara or Sònia or Judit, and they go out with boys who take them to the gym and know nothing about all this. Or do know and stay out of it. They live with their parents. They go to college.

He let his eyelids drop again, letting his hands take the lead, he felt her and went to her sex as was his wont— headfirst into the river—and the shock was as imminent as the tree trunk was for the two brothers. Knock up your daughter, make her a mother and grandmother, take her out of the running. Lives kept coming and going and now a new one shows up. The accident hadn't cut short a long life, but rather two short lives that had yet to branch out: pure miscarriages. It was nothing. He put his hand on her sex, proof that the living are made to be with each other, the bodies themselves deformed to fit together—needing to talk, sometimes, on their own. Not even pregnancy lets us escape that. It was death, what brought them together. All bodies, dead or alive: plants, rocks, horses, and mountains. They followed the sway of sex, the movement of skeletons, as if it could shut off their consciousness and give comfort in the company of a shared night. But the more he wanted to get those thoughts out of his head, the more they imposed themselves. It seemed he might shake them off with a violent lurch, but he knew he couldn't, his head was loaded down with years, with floors and stairwells, each day the same as the last, all the boredom that must have started one day—perhaps when he signed his first contract to work at the bank—the desperate life of an older man, everything ending, just remnants, Mondays waiting for Fridays, Fridays waiting for Mondays, and, thank you ever so much; when he retires he won't even have that. The dead fell from the trees onto the boredom of the living, and every once in a while a muffled clarification: the temptation of suicide, sometimes like a compassionate light and sometimes like a bitter, soiling cowardice. Waiting behind soundproof glass and waiting, not doing anything but waiting. Meanwhile, on top of him—with reins and a crop, sinking spurs into his belly, riding him at a gallop until he's worn out—is his own tedium, the exhaustion of him as a person.

But now the tedium had been cracked open. He had wished for a car accident a thousand times, as a reward for all those trips to Vidreres. And those two poor kids had the accident. The two young brothers had the accident. They'd mocked him. Here he had the consolation of the girl they left behind. If she hadn't showed up in those wings, maybe Ernest would have told her what he wanted: pain. Not wings, but shoes. Shoes leaving tread marks, rubber tracks on his back, the conscious braking. A payment for being here, for remaining, for having escaped the car in place of the brother who was driving.

He filled his hands with the girl's flesh, and his eagerness was because the dead wanted sex: it was a child's game, religious, familiar, and worn. He opened his eyes and finished undressing her, and he didn't care anymore about being under the sheets. Guilt is the marrow in life's bones, the only consistent thing in life, blessed, beloved guilt, the material we are made of, the dead, children, parents of the dead, their deaths a gift from our unconscious, and it was becoming urgent that he ejaculate. He ran his hand over the girl's straight hair, shiny and clean, with the grooves from the comb visible, still damp, and he looked around the bed for satellites of her, pieces of clothing, her purse, dresses, shoes—the shoes he would have liked to feel on the skin of his back, hard and painful enough to keep him from thinking—the vanity case, the silvery cell phone, the short jacket that would end up at the back of the closet and then in the trash, and which she'd see someday, when she was his age, in the photographs of her youth, like his daughters will see him in photos after he's dead.

So distract yourself, celebrate the boys' destruction, celebrate with their parents as if the boys were your daughters; swallow the incest, the necrophilia, it's over, they won't die again, move toward her, sink yourself deep inside.

A thrust for his life in the office, two thrusts for the boys' lives, and one each for the short jacket, the earrings, the wings, a thrust for the ivy tattoo on her back, and another for not crying, for life to live, for life impossible to live, for the lure of life that kills you and nourishes you, for the guilt of feeling guilty, for the shouts and the chains, for life where the only joy is in deception, for life sunk in muddy quagmires filled with drowning, crying babies, for life that knows no pain or rapture, and a thrust for each closing coffin; he had to ejaculate, to rid himself of that intention, and he asked the girl to give him a hand.

Had the dead boys been released from inside him with his orgasm? Can there be consciousness of the unconscious? She got up, grabbed a towel, and left the room. She wasn't that professional. She left the men alone too soon.

He heard the voices of Miqui and Cloe on the other side of the door, and a laugh. Water ran through the pipes. Marga was showering. She would come back into the room soon to get dressed. He couldn't allow himself to sleep, but his eyelids were heavy. He'd drift off, he wouldn't think about anything, he would melt...

He heard a door open and gave a start. It was the trucker coming into the bedroom, buckling his belt.

He covered his belly. He sat up against the headboard. The trucker extended a hand: "Buddy, I gotta go."

"You're going?"

"I'm leaving you in good hands. For a hundred euros, you couldn't ask for more."

"Do you get a commission?"

"I don't want any misunderstandings."

Ernest got dressed and got the money. He took a last look at the jacket and wings on the floor. He rushed. He didn't want to see her again. He would give the money to the other girl. He would get home, have dinner, a shower, and go to bed. Maybe he'd have a bath. The next day, he'd go back to the office. He would start the week over. The truck heading off blended into the persistent sound of the shower. He wondered if he'd gotten her that dirty.

As he left the house, the water was still running through the pipes.

After a few kilometers he stopped the car. The wheels skidded as if it had been raining for weeks and the highway was flooded with mud. He got out of the car and found the asphalt soft, but it wasn't mud, it was flesh. He looked around. Mountains, trees, and houses of flesh. Blood flowing in the rivers, the clouds were blubber, everyone had gotten out of their cars, there were worms everywhere.

THE EXTRATERRESTRIAL

I

He yawned, let his pajamas drop to the floor, and put on the sweater he'd worn the day before, with wisps of hay still on the elbows. It was eleven in the morning, and he had been up past five chatting online with a girl in Seville, a nice set of jugs if the photo was actually her—and if not, whoever was typing in her name had good taste, they'd chosen a very warm, summery photo. Even though now it was winter, the girl in the picture wore a red tank top, the sides open in wide ovals from the shoulder to the waist, with no hint of a bra, the neckline revealing incredible orbs of flesh that lifted the fabric. The best jugs on the market. If they weren't hers, they must have been chosen by a man or a lesbian. But that didn't matter, you went online to be altruistic, to find and offer generosity, to forgive from the get-go, to give yourself over to the gratuitousness of a limitless, empty planet devoid of responsibility—created by man, though, and therefore not infinite, just beyond your reach. The Internet didn't have nature's independence; tied to humans, it could only be fantasy up to a certain point. And it contained a world of altruism—you could be talking to the scum of the earth, to the worst criminals, serial killers, and terrorists, bad people who, if they caught you in the forest, would crush you without thinking twice—but that's just how the Internet is, it redeems and purifies them. And how many imposters do we come across every day without even realizing? Who wasn't covering up their belly, the folds we want to hide even from ourselves, since we can't go around showing them? But if all you get from the imposters is a sham, what sham are we even talking about? The mask is the truth, they don't cheat you on the Internet: whores who don't charge aren't whores.

He posted different photographs depending on the day, out of generosity. He used the name "Miqui" so he felt more identified with the photos, and he updated them depending on his mood. He had folders full of faces to choose from. The best photo was of an executive with very short blond hair and a gleaming new shirt. Chicks drooled over guys like that. It had taken him months to find a photo that fit his personality so well. Our outsides and our insides never match up. The earth is a chaos of seven billion outer shells and seven billion personalities; faces never perfectly fit their owners, souls and bodies do their own thing; the dead, the living, the young, and the old in a tangle of locations and moments, all chaos and orgy. Who was that blond jerk whose face Miqui'd swiped? What country was he from? What year was the photo taken? Maybe the blond was bald now. And what if that exact blond guy had a personality that matched Miqui's face? What if the blond guy's personality—from inside Miqui's shell—was punching and kicking at the walls of his prison of a face? Who knew what son of a bitch was wearing the blond guy's façade. Who knows whose boobs those really were or what kind of narcissist hid behind the sweet smile of the waitress at the social club yesterday.

They can do face transplants. They transplant the whole kit and caboodle: the forehead, eyebrows, eyelids, nostrils, cheeks and lips, moles, chin. They resuscitate the dead face for the blank head of a poor wretch who's lost his. They take off what's left of the old face, file down the bones, and slip a new face on like a sock. The transplantee washes it every morning in front of the mirror. He's the same, he just looks different. His face sweats or is cold like always, it itches or it stings, he feels the sun beating down on it, he feels the rain falling on it. He gets blackheads, inflamed pimples, his beard grows ... but wait a second: whose beard is that? His hairs and his tears go through someone else's skin. If it's a woman who receives the transplant, who does she put her lipstick, eye shadow, foundation, and sunglasses on? More masks atop the mask. Her boyfriend doesn't know who he's caressing. Who's he kissing if he kisses her on the cheek? The flayed skull of a cadaver buried a thousand kilometers away. And when he kisses her on the mouth, whose lips does his tongue slip through?

There's a whole business around it. They bring faces from far away, just in case, but they can't bring them from too far off, from some continent with other races; for example, they can't put an Asian face on a European body. But the faces travel to and fro, there are markets, they organize swaps and fairs on sporting fields, with stands filled with faces, butcher shops of masks, wholesale or retail—How many would you like, doctor? That makes a kilo—and right now trucks like his, filled with faces, drive down the streets, roads, and expressways. There are stockpiles of faces traveling on planes, trains, and boats. In portside warehouses, containers filled with faces wait for a semi to come pick them up. Flesh masks hang on hooks in refrigerated rooms beneath clinics and hospitals, surgeons handle them with surgical gloves, spin them on two fingers like pizza dough to air them out so they'll give a bit as they're sewn on the head. There are catalogues of masks, categories, supply, demand, swaps... You like this one? It'll suit you perfectly. Would you like to see the photo of its previous owner to get an idea of what you'll look like?

The young widow from yesterday. The fiancée of one of the accident victims. She goes abroad on vacation. Walking alone down a street, she sees a familiar face. It can't be. Her heart skips a beat. It can't be. The face smiles at her. Her lover's face on a stranger's body. Surprised to see her looking at him like that, the boy comes over and speaks to her in English.

Who do the faces belong to? And the bodies? Whose are they?

The blond executive's mug was the best one he had, but he changed it as easily as—depending on his mood—he changed the picture in his mind of the person whose fingers typed the words that appeared on his screen from some corner of cyberspace. Quick replies filled with good intentions and good vibes emerged on the luminous pond of the screen amid an exasperating chaos of multicolored ads and last-minute offers for porn sites and online sex shops, cyber casinos, airlines, shops that sold tires and spare truck parts, antivirus programs, video games . . . In the midst of that mess of invasive little pop-up windows, there was an oasis of altruism and warmth, of serenity and trust, a tear in the fabric of selfish demands.

What's wrong, Miqui?

You really think so?

Do you want me to explain what happened to me?

I understand, Miqui.

I'm so sorry, Miqui.

Life's a bitch.

We all have our moments.

Tell me, Miqui, I want to know.

Words climbing out of the abyss, company. The screen flickered like a star at the heart of a dark room in an apartment on a carless street in Sils, a fading star, around which the room's furnishings slowly revolved, the unmade bed whose skirt dragged on the ground, the chair with a mountain of clothes to iron and fold, sleeves and pant legs hanging between chair legs, the cardboard box with the empty cans from the beers he occasionally got up to get from the kitchen . . . the cylindrical basket with the overflowing bag of dirty laundry . . .

The small table was another orbiting planet, with the unplugged clock radio, green lamp with a burnt-out bulb, and little drawers that he never opened filled with coins, cards, pens, maps of cities he'd traveled to a thousand years ago, papers, photographs, and torn concert tickets . . . There was a poster the mechanic had given him, pinned up right beside the window with its blinds drawn, a blown-up photo of the latest model of a Mercedes Atego, red like his, and with a crane and a cargo bed, but his was already twenty years old. The mechanic must have thought he could buy it, that he'd fall in love and do anything to have it; he must have taken him for a truck nut, crazy for engines. Miqui knew a few guys like that. The mechanic must have thought he'd ask for a loan—not that they'd give it to him—because his Atego was a wreck. He was always having to fix it, one patch over the next, and the mechanic had told him he could buy a new one with all he spent on repairs. Sure, he had thought. In my next life. The Atego's nose stuck out from the middle of the stretch of wall, through a frame of white thumbtacks . . . The poster was curling slowly, puffing out slightly like a shifting sail, a carefully maneuvering truck . . .

The closet's open door was like a dissected wing, lined with photographs of top models, the most attractive faces of ten years past, which had yellowed in the photographs; they'd dried out on paper just as they'd dried out in real life, expired models, past their sell-by date . . . And on the top shelf of the closet there was a case with a shotgun inside, above the bar of empty hangers—he only had two shirts hung up, two ridiculous shirts he never wore—the case was half hidden amid a pile of notebooks and textbooks from high school, a dinged trophy he had won in a school literary contest, and a racket . . .

When he was feeling good he would post the photo of a tennis player with curly hair, a guy younger than him, damp with sweat after winning a game, with two days of beard growth, clean, smiling, sporty. In his best moments, Miqui felt like that. It was like pulling back a curtain and discovering himself improved. He would confess after an endless chat session, once the chick convinced him to meet up to have a coffee or go to bed together. Then it was time to say, "I'm not the guy in the photo," but the conversation had already gone too far for her to really mind, and she would convince herself that she didn't really care; anyway, the photo she'd posted wasn't her, either. Or it was her but twenty years ago, or looking taller and more attractive, or with longer hair. On the web, everyone was very generous.

It was hard to resist the temptation to get together with someone. He had to offset the gravity of the bodies behind these conversations. Bodies have gravity, without gravity people would float off the planet, only rooted plants would be left on Earth, the sea's water would scatter throughout the universe, and the fish would float, dead, among the planets. He had printed out a red stop sign with the words MEETING UP underneath, and taped it to his keyboard. The girls he chatted with were far away, in Barcelona at least, and he did short-haul transport, when he had work. But even if he did drive long distances, he wouldn't have listened to the other truckers who suggested he get in touch with chicks in the places where he was headed; he didn't want to pay for a hotel or sex. They insisted, but he wasn't convinced. The real angels lived in Guatemala or Galicia. He ruled out chatting with anyone under twenty-five, and he chose them by their location, always at least five hundred kilometers away. They couldn't understand why he didn't want to meet up, they confused the generosity of the web with the self-serving generosity of the world outside; they brought the virus of their miserable lives to the Internet.

There was no need to take it all the way. Approach your prey, follow her tracks, get a sense of her, sniff her out, just play. He could have written manuals. There are shy victims and clever victims, bold ones and enigmatic ones, it was different every time: there could be a camera and virtual sex, but never a get-together. People got together out of laziness. It wasn't that he had a problem hooking up. Miqui didn't look too out of his element at a nightclub, the hunting ground whose only ruses were dim lights and alcohol, among teenagers with wide foreheads, like bulls. It was in one of those large rooms with dark ceilings, fake clouds, and music that he had met Cèlia, ten years ago. But it was different in chat rooms. Chatting was altruistic. The chat was a haven. The layers of idealization you wrapped the other person in would always ruin any later get-together.

He met Marga and Cloe via their little show one morning. He was chatting with one of those understanding souls—her photograph was of a fuckable teenager, although the chat said 30+—when a window with a red frame opened up beside an ad for bargain trucks, and there were the two girls in blue lingerie looking at him through a camera and waving to attract his attention. Could they be watching him? He had no way of being sure. He hadn't poked out the camera above his laptop screen, and he hadn't taped it over. Then he heard them through the speakers.

"Can you hear us? Hello? Do you hear us?" they asked in Spanish.

Did they want to know if he, specifically, could hear them, or was it a message they sent out to thousands of men like him, typing in thousands of dark rooms? They were stuck behind the plastic screen, making troubling gestures toward him, as if they were drowning, as if they needed him or had an important message to convey to him, as if the bed they were on was a hospital bed where they were spending the final hours of their lives—or: We've been held hostage in this garage for three years, forced to do this, now we have a quick chance to talk, they've gone out, please, help us!

He typed "perfectly" and then added "loud and clear." One girl was hugging the other from behind and had a tattoo of ivy and was wearing wings. It wasn't recorded. They started talking to him. They were Internet whores. He kept chatting with the teenage-photo woman as he watched the girls in the little side window out of the corner of his eye. He could place an order for any of the dirty thoughts running through his head just by sending text messages. Opportunists. They had caught him horny and distracted. Finally, he got rid of the chat, unbuttoned his pants, and when he was at his most defenseless, Marga suggested they meet up. They were much closer than he'd realized, they worked out of Lloret.

He opened the other door of the closet and pulled the case off the shelf. It was a wooden case with a leather strap and inside was a shotgun, in pieces. What's a shotgun worth? It made no sense to pawn it for clothes; you have to really be scraping bottom before clothes are more useful to you than a shotgun.

He put the case on the bed, opened it, and studied the pieces. They smelled of gunpowder and grease. They looked new considering their age, dark, shiny, and anesthetized by the padded interior: the black barrel, the varnished wood of the butt, the cylindrical cartridges with their purplish shells and golden caps, the white instruction pamphlet with the Beretta logo he'd used to learn to put it together years ago. Without Ahmed, he could now carry it under the seat in his truck, feel its energy in his balls, or, even better, hang it from the ceiling: a cascade of firepower over his skull, a radiation shower of wood, iron, and gunpowder. A man on foot wasn't the same as a man in a truck. A man with his hands in his pockets wasn't the same as a man with a shotgun.

He thought about Cindy again. Maybe he was falling in love; he really wanted to see her again. And it wasn't even springtime. He had met three fuckable chicks in just one day: Cindy, the widow—with the morbid appeal of that black dress against her milky skin—and that little whore with the ringlets. She wouldn't last long where she was. He'd have to hurry if he wanted a taste of her. Have her come up into the cab, sit her down on top of him, and ask her to glance up at the ceiling while he was screwing her. Why? she would ask. What's there?

"You're giving me the truck but not the shotgun?" Miqui had complained to his father.

"It was a present from my mother. It was my grandfather's."

"That was so you could defend us. You don't have to do that anymore."

But he didn't really know what his great-grandfather was doing with a shotgun, or why it had been in his father's room for so many years. He only knew about its existence after his mother died. Every evening, after locking the truck in the lumber warehouse, his father picked him up at his Aunt Marta's house. Aunt Marta would get Miqui from school at five and give him a snack. His father arrived later and walked him home down streets that smelled of fried food, carrying a basket filled with the dinner his aunt had prepared for them.

One night, his father was late. His aunt sat by the phone, but his father didn't call. He ate dinner with her. Later, on the way home, his father's hand was trembling and sweaty, and when they arrived he asked him to wait in the dining room instead of going to bed. He came out of his bedroom with the wooden case. It was the first time Miqui saw it. His father placed it on the table and had the shotgun assembled in five seconds—it would take him five minutes now, if he could do it at all.

"When you're scared," he said, "remember this."

It was he who had been scared that night, more than his father. He was a twelve-year-old boy, and he liked the world better without shotguns. A decade and a half later, when, after the accident, his father gave him the truck, Miqui asked him for the shotgun too. The world was better but more complicated than when he was a child.

Now he put it together, placed the cartridges in his pocket, put the case away again, and took the gun to the dining room. Yesterday's dinner plates were still on the table. He took aim at a bottle. Then he slowly shifted the barrel and aimed at the pile of dirty plates in the sink. The shotgun wasn't loaded. He fired. He took aim, fired, and cocked it again without ammunition. When he got tired of playing, he leaned it against the table with the barrel toward the ceiling. He cleared the table and swept the breadcrumbs up off the floor. A while back they had fired the cleaning lady, a short, stocky Bolivian woman, with the same sort of body he'd expect to find under Cindy's clothes—South American chicks came in packages with short expiration dates. She'd vanished from town just like Ahmed, and now the house was filled with dirty clothes, they were everywhere. His father just lay about all day. If he hadn't let himself get ripped off, they'd be able to hire someone to clean and cook once in a while, or he could live in a nursing home. But the banks worked together to prey on the weakest, the most helpless, on people who felt they were protected, people who had grown trusting over the course of their lives. And when they had them where they wanted them, they gave them what they deserved. There were about twenty people in town who'd been fleeced; every once in a while they held meetings, but Miqui and his father never went, why bother, when it mortified his father and he already knew there was nothing they could do.

There was a bit of milk left in the carton, but he wasn't sure if it was sour, so he put it in his coffee along with four teaspoons of sugar. He picked up the shotgun again and laid it on the table. The old man was on the other side of the door, awake on the double bed. Every morning he turned on the TV and waited in his room until Miqui cleared out. His son didn't return home until the night or early morning. He spent his days watching the same programs: talk shows and news programs that confirmed it was best not to go out. On the days when Miqui stayed home, he made his father get out of bed. He would shout at him, and soon the man would stick his head out of his room, his pajamas bloated by his diaper. He'd drag himself to the bathroom like the skeleton of a frightened rabbit. The smell of piss wafting through the house. He washed and changed his own diaper, for the moment, but that was a ticking time bomb.

He never went out. He never saw anyone. He didn't talk to Miqui. Just television. It was his way of complaining, letting himself drop, depressed, upon his son. Old people are selfish, their weakness makes them distrusting, like the old man with the cane in Vidreres the day before, wanting to look pitiful, still milking a war he'd seen from afar as a schoolboy. What more could young people today ask for than a war and at least the hope of winning it? They consoled themselves by massacring soldiers on a PlayStation or Wii. They couldn't prove themselves out in the world, they weren't like him, who had known how to make a life for himself, they were penned in like industrial pigs or hens or cows; today, housing developments were warehouses for young people, buildings to store them in, stalls with the lights on twenty-four hours a day, each with their girl or boy or group of siblings inside, facing a screen like lambs at the trough. He knew a ton of people like that, always connected when he got online, always available on the Internet but only on the Internet, he had friends from high school who ended up settling in to live in the virtual world instead of the physical, gravitational one—exiled to the hidden world, all tangled up together in a mess of circuits, chained by Wi-Fi to their computers, tablets, and cell phones, hypnotized, captured by the spider who lived with them. These millennials, young people who didn't study or work, who couldn't do either. They're born already knowing, the mutation has occurred, the youngest ones have adapted. Sometimes he envied them. He had to struggle with the truck to make ends meet. He was part of a hinge generation between the old people who had everything and the young who had nothing, but because they had nothing, they were spared from anxiety. There were still girls in the chat rooms who tried to get together with him. They asked to see him. They wanted to meet. They wanted to go out. They wanted to extricate themselves. But how could they survive out there, when there's nothing left for them?

It was the fault of sons of bitches like his father. Who had brand-new Ategos like the one in the poster? When he passed by a restaurant—a date-night restaurant, not like the cheap one on the side of the highway he went to the day before—and looked through the window, he only saw old people inside, big-bellied guys like the banker from Vidreres. How far was that guy, Ernest, from retirement? He could settle into a little house overlooking the sea to live out the rest of his years. But old folks don't retire anymore. They had extended the retirement age. Why should they retire, when everything was hunky-dory? The old folks had good jobs and salaries, they had the dough, they had gotten there first. There are old people who are dirt poor, scum of the earth like his father, and there always will be, but what was over for good was young people with money or the possibility of making any. Everything was taken, starting with the illegal businesses. Sure, chicks could still be whores, being young was a definite advantage there, and the clever ones worked in secret like Marga and Cloe. But the restaurants he used to go to with his father every Sunday before the recession, had suddenly disappeared, the restaurants filled with young couples celebrating the signing of their forty-year mortgages, with tables reserved weeks in advance, the triumph of all that culinary crap, the chefs who were on TV every day, those bastards that served up mind-boggling dishes, who brought on mass poisoning with their white surgeons' uniforms and Santoku knives, their cleavers and hands soaking wet from rummaging around in the guts of young people, their raw material, the base of their dishes, yes, the chefs were in on it, they were a key piece of the scam, they helped to cook the books. Until, all of a sudden, there were no more enology courses, no more silicone breast and lip implants for teenagers, no more trips to New York and the Caribbean for the kids, no more bricklayers' assistants with 4x4s, no more everyone having a second home. The property that was supposed to ensure your future, in the end turned into a life sentence, the scam of the century. Everything was over for the young, just like that. They were as confident as their parents, but ended up being the butt of the joke—last one's a rotten egg—and now the good cars were for the old, the cruises were for the old, the expensive clothing shops, the jewels, the spas, the massages, the high-class whores were for the old. The old folks had had their youth, but they'd had such a good time they'd come back for seconds, and thirds, and keep coming back for more. They were living their thousandth youth; they were bombproof, they'd aged well but hadn't done anything more, squandering money like the young—they were role models in that—but the properties, the businesses, the companies, the posts, and the banks were theirs. They were living it up right in front of the noses of their children, grandchildren, and great-grandchildren. Because they could. They'd leave their bones as an inheritance. Farewell and good-bye. You can have this piece-of-shit world, here's your embezzlement, your ruined country, the political system we turned into a fucking cage, ten thousand Fukushimas, and a hundred thousand warehouses of mortal remains. You can keep it, enjoy! Farewell and screw you! Those two poor kids from the car wreck had gotten out in time. There was that. Old folks who would launch a nuclear holocaust if they knew they had to die tomorrow. Die. Them? No fucking way were they gonna die. They wouldn't die tomorrow. They wouldn't ever die, the kings of the world would survive like roaches and rats, you'd find them everywhere; two kids cash in their chips against a tree on the side of the road, and who do you find there the next day, pondering it, musing over it, philosophizing? A banker. Then who shows up, on foot, brimming with life, getting a little exercise like someone going to the gym, with his cane and his stories from the Pleistocene epoch? Some three-hundred-year-old piece of shit. Every new medicine extends old people's lives, so they have time to find another cure to keep them alive until the next discovery. They run the pharmaceutical industry, they specialize in defeating the cancers of old age, geriatric oncology was making leaps and bounds, eternally healthy prostates, skin, breasts, and colons, replacement parts; soon they'd cure Alzheimer's; soon the old would watch the young pass them by, soon the young would be the old and the old would be the young—thirty-two-year-old old people, like him, trying to survive by rummaging through the dump, wrinkled by unemployment and bad news, gutted, playing dominoes on the Internet while outside hundred-year-old young people sunbathed all day long, and spent their nights leaping and dancing in the discos—when you see someone with tender skin and impeccable teeth, colorful clothes, long, shiny hair, full of health and joie de vivre, they'll be old. Everything will be the same as ever, but with the young watching from the margins with their hands out. The old get beauty treatments and operate on their faces and breasts, they go to the gym, they take Viagra, they reproduce on their own—sixty-year-old women with kids, ninety-year-old grandmas buying wombs for hire or even giving birth themselves—they haven't renounced anything. And the day they discover an immortality pill they can get rid of the young without regrets. They'll have gotten what they wanted. It's a fact of life, they will say, the planet has to regulate itself, there isn't room for everyone, and our font of experience is essential. Then the young will just be in the way; they should have been prepared. It was only a question of time. They're in charge, and the young are just some poor aliens; they control the governments and they run the system, they would get rid of the young without a second thought.

He picked up the shotgun and aimed it at the bedroom door. His old man was on the other side, lying in bed with his eyes open, waiting for him to finally leave. The music from the television slipped out under the door. His father was slow and silent, every day he walked, shoeless, in pajamas and socks, to the bathroom, before getting dressed. If he opened the door now he'd find a barrel in his face. He would have another heart attack. Would anything really change if he were in a wheelchair? Or would it be worse?

He could play like that with his father and yet didn't abandon him, didn't disappear and let him die alone, peacefully. He had the feeling that he wasn't completely in control of the extremes, that he only had a handle on what was within certain limits. Both kindness and wickedness lay outside of his jurisdiction. But that didn't mean they weren't there: they had ways of crossing the border on their own, they knew hidden paths, secret tunnels, they entered him illegally, saints disguised as Adolf Hitler, scorpions among the harmless silverware in the kitchen drawer, and he didn't realize until it was too late.

His father's story wouldn't end well. Knowing the end, why continue? He pulled two shells out of his pocket and loaded the shotgun. The cartridge cap was dented; the gun was at least twenty years old.

You made me and raised me; you are responsible for me.

He kept aiming until his arms got tired. Then he lowered the shotgun and put it back down on the table. There was a bit of thick yellowish sludge at the bottom of his mug, a sweet paste that would have to be poured down the drain.

"Papa," he said, without raising his voice. "I'm off. I'll leave this for you on the table."

He only meant the shotgun, but animals sense danger. It rains and the snails come out of their holes, to save themselves from the water, they climb up plants, little birds chirp nonstop as they fall from their nest, and even a shitty little ant will spin around like a lunatic when it senses death. His father had heard him, he was old not stupid, and the door opened.

"Mind telling me what you're doing with that?" his father asked. "You can take it with you, alright? You can throw it into the woods, you hear me? I don't ever want to see it again!"

I was playing with the shotgun. It went off. It would be

the prosecutor's word against mine. And who wants to kill his own father? And why? They would let him off precisely because it was his father.

What difference is there between any old guy and your father? Why should it be any less natural to want to blow your father away? Children have power over their parents, because children are the only ones who know the truth about them. They have a lot of information—not only genetic—they have knowledge, they know better than anyone what's going on inside their parents. It's not parents who know their children—parents know their kids through themselves, like a replica, not an original, and anyway, they've gotten too old, they're muddled up, can't keep things straight—it's the children who know their parents: they have inherited the secret codes, the incriminating information, the definitive proof.

If he left the shotgun on the table for his father, was there any possibility that he would use it? None. His father had always known where the shotgun was. Miqui put on the safety, covered it with his jacket, and left the apartment. As he went down the stairs —there was still time to go back—an embolism started to form in his brain, the pool of blood that would have emerged from his father's pajamas; blood that spread over the floor, so clean he could see himself in it, blood of his blood drawn in blood, father and son, each mirroring the other.

II

The truck was waiting for him at the back of the lumber warehouse. He jumped into the cab, put the shotgun down on the seat beside him, started the engine, and went out onto the street with the feeling that he was opening tunnels with the nose of his truck.

He floated over life's miseries. He could see abandoned yards behind the fences, with yellow grass and pools covered with blue tarps waiting for summer. He could see into the houses through their windows and searched among the shadows for the silhouette of a married woman, welcoming in her nest. He extended his hand and touched the cold metal of the shotgun, gave it his warmth, made it his, real, sensitive, and powerful as an erection. He was against emasculated life: only discomfort and discord opened your eyes, you had to set up a disconnect with the world if you didn't have one, a personality that allowed you to separate yourself so you could see it. But you also had to have the courage to accept the world, accept the bribe of light-filled days like today. Days when you pull back the curtains and the world is fucking awesome. Pull back the curtains and find it crystal clear, set up perfectly for you to live in, all of it in perfect harmony with you.

He had a CD of romantic ballads, Celine Dion, R.E.M., Mariah Carey, songs to get you in the mood that he'd downloaded a few years back, the music of the moments that gave life meaning. He put it on and imagined himself the day before, the truck seen from the heavens like in a film, the bird's-eye view of a boat transporting bales of hay, a merchant ship with its deck covered in golden containers, big gold ingots crossing the smooth sea of the fields of Vidreres. Every day was harder, every day it cost him more to fill the tank, it was true, but most of the other truckers had it worse; he had seen it coming and had come up with a plan in time, printing up some cards and giving them out before business was a total bust: MIQUEL TRUCKING / TRANSPORT ALL TYPES. He had to put up with his father, but it could be a lot worse. His father had stagnated, but he'd been saved by mixing it up; with Ahmed, anytime they could, they alternated another trip to the construction site with some other kind of transport job: a piano for a promoter, some friend of a friend moving houses, the kind of jobs that at the time were of no interest to the construction truckers, who would only take them on for exorbitant sums. He'd gotten clients by handing out cards and posting ads on the Internet, and so now he could just as easily be asked to transport refrigerators for a store as five hundred folding chairs for an event, six tons of dirt, dead trees and shrubs cleared out of a garden, a few hundred boxes of potatoes, a load of hay bales, or a small boat.

He wasn't the only one who suffered attacks of optimism.

In recent months, balconies and windows had filled with independence flags, and the local center-right and center-left governments had hoisted Catalan flags at the traffic circles leading into their towns. He saw them constantly in his truck, some bright and new and others already faded by sun and rain. The cowardly Catalans were now lifting their heads, counting each other, and discovering there were enough. It's not that they'd gotten any braver: the enemy was off his game. They pointed each other out, recognized each other. For every real estate agency or bank that closed, a half-dozen independentist flags appeared in windows and on balconies. Near every flag was a sign or two that read FOR SALE. Apartments for sale. Commercial spaces, industrial warehouses. The whole country for sale, like a whore.

They consoled themselves by hanging up flags; he knew a few people who were trapped by their mortgages, title-holders of apartments filled with useless rooms, owners of second homes they'd never pay off in towns they'd only been to two or three times in their lives. They couldn't visit their properties because they couldn't afford the gas. For ten years everybody was rich. What a scam. Four bricks slapped together on any open patch of ground was the business of the century. There was some for everybody. You walked over diamond mines. People bought apartments like they were buying shoes—every street had a real estate agency. Everything was a great opportunity. You found brochures with residential offerings at the hairdressers', in bars, in dentists' waiting rooms, and in public bathrooms. The local governments kept enlarging the area zoned for construction, everyone was lining their pockets. Miqui could do seven trips a day carrying construction materials. Maçanet, Sils, Vidreres, Riudarenes, Santa Coloma de Farners, big towns inland, this armpit of the world was filled with cranes, giant crosses for the crucifixion no one was expecting. The politicians came out on TV to say that everything was going gangbusters. Buy! Get into debt! The Catalan president, a socialist, when everything was already starting to crumble, still kept it up: Buy! Spend! What bastards. It was part of the business. Now, along the road you saw the last construction projects, stopped. The cranes still there for a few months before they started to take them down, whether or not the buildings were finished. There wasn't a single one left. Just construction sites. Concrete skeletons. Abandoned streets with sidewalks, streetlamps, and trash cans, lots ready for houses that would never be built. Housing developments in the middle of the woods that would be covered over by vegetation like prehistoric cities. Houses and apartments for sale on the one hand, people evicted on the other. Young people living with their parents or emigrating. A real model society. And now they were talking about independence, now that they'd gone bankrupt.

Who had set all this up? Passing through the square he saw retirees stooped over golden pétanque balls, the lines they made etching tangled squiggles. Selfish old men…with their sun hats, they lived the same lives as the retired Germans who came here to live like kings while our young people had to emigrate to Germany to work in their Nazi factories. Only the old people were left. Buses filled with teenagers set off for Mindelheim, Dresden, and Frankfurt; they signed agreements to deport kids for professional training. They would never return. It was for the young people's own good, according to their parents and grandparents, but the truth was their pensions depended on it. They went to say good-bye to their children and grandchildren at the bus, and then they came back to continue the game.

What could you expect from towns like Sils? That's the way it was. Some car accidents, some flashers, some embezzlements, some robberies at some farmhouses, some pederasts, and a few crimes of passion. Married women whose kids were at school chatted all day with men like him, until they were found out by their husbands, the ones who had jobs to support the family, who couldn't devote their time to such amorous refinement. Who knew what fantasies they entertained about their wives' affairs after those wives informed them they were leaving them for someone else. The first thing that went through the husband's head was to run to the kitchen and find a knife. There was a case every year, in Sils or Riudarenes or wherever; not long ago it was a policeman in Caldes, his wife had left him and gone to live with her sister: the cop slit his sister-in-law's throat in the yard, in front of his nieces—It's your fault! You filled her head with lies! Then he stabbed his wife, but immediately regretted it: he drove her to the emergency room where they saved her life; meanwhile, the sister-in-law bled to death as her daughters screamed and cried.

He turned off the music. In the Serramagra industrial park, also empty, its large buildings covered with FOR SALE / FOR RENT signs, an independence flag waved above a concrete wall covered in graffiti. He stopped the truck in front of the gate. He honked the horn, and Isma came out to open it for him. The walls enclosed a large lot filled with piles of tires. There were hundreds, piled up by size: truck, car, and touring motorcycle. Isma was a guy his age. He made his living from his contacts with mechanics and dealers. When a junker came down the pipeline they called him and gave him a couple of hours to switch the tires for some completely worn out ones from the shop. For Isma, the accident in Vidreres was a business opportunity.

Today, Miqui hadn't come to get tires for his truck, but rather twenty or thirty useless ones for a moving job. There was a huge mountain in the middle of the yard, and on top hung the independentist flag he'd seen from outside, shiny and new at the top of a long pole.

"I have to go pick up a boat," Miqui said. "The owner hasn't paid rent on the mooring for months, and they don't have a boat trailer. It'll fit on the flatbed, but I need some cushioning for the base and sides."

They threw some tires onto the truck bed. Then they spread them out on the floor and tied some to the walls.

"Any news from Ahmed?" asked Isma.

"He must be in Morocco."

"He's lucky he can leave this piece-of-shit country."

"Yeah, like the rats."

"Fuck off, you antisocial jerk. You want to stay here, don't you? Look what I do to make a living. I had to sell my motorcycle. All I have is this shitty van to go pick up tires. It's even older than your truck. I sold off my car for next to nothing and then my bike. Not you, you're not married. I walk here every day, I've got enough dough for three or four months, and then it's over: I'll have to sell the apartment at a loss, and

I'll be lucky to find a buyer. What do you think they'll give me for it? They're lying in wait. I'm in hot water up to my neck and all because of fucking Spain and this den of thieves. Holy hell, Miqui, they screwed us every chance they got, and now they're squeezing the last bit of life out of us; soon we won't even be able to complain, because we won't have any strength left. They've fucked up my whole life, and yours, and your father's too—they made out like bandits. I don't understand where you get your patience. Look at the king and his family. Millions and millions of euros in their pockets, the whole government is corrupt, everyone here is on the take . . . everyone except us, we're the ones who pay the price. I really don't get you. They fucking screwed your father! They stole everything; they've been making trains nonstop so they can get the commissions, high-speed rail in a country that needs to keep buying cars, for fuck's sake, they don't care that they're ruining our industry, they couldn't care less, they've killed the hen that lays golden eggs . . . look at me. You think I deserve this? You know how hard I've worked? We've got to open our eyes, Miqui. I'm up to my neck. I can get by for four months, tops, then I've got nowhere to go except back to my parents', and Tere and the boy will go to her parents', because we won't all fit in my in-laws' apartment . . . We need to move toward independence, everybody knows that, and fast."

"They'll line you all up against the wall in front of a firing squad."

"Fuck you. Europe won't let that happen."

"No, they'll rush to save you all. That's why you put up the flags. Never seen such a thing. You guys have put up your own targets."

"Now you're telling me you're afraid. You? You want a flag? Why don't you put a flag in your cab? Maybe you've got it wrong and they'll shoot everyone who doesn't have one. We're past fear. Young people have nothing to lose, and a lot to gain."

"Young people never get off the Internet. They have no idea about the world."

"If we have to defend ourselves, we will. I have a 3-D printer. You know what that is, right? You can make a gun."

"A plastic gun? You're an idiot," said Miqui, opening the passenger-side door so Isma could see his shotgun. "I want to hang it from the roof. Can you help me?"

"Are you getting ready?"

"I'm always getting ready."

He passed Llagostera on the left, with its church above a row of houses, then went down the Alou glen and entered the Aro valley. In Castell d'Aro they'd put up a Catalan flag as large as a swimming pool. It overshadowed the valley and waved in the tramontane, the dry, luminous, cleansing north wind that burnished the coast. Against the backdrop of the sea you could already see the small white skyscrapers of Platja d'Aro, the summer apartments that were now empty. He turned onto the tourist stretch, filled with deserted shop windows and closed bars. He crossed the Ridaura bridge and reached the canals of Port d'Aro. They had built up the whole area in recent years, putting in a complex with movie theaters, supermarkets, a gas station, a hotel, and new apartment buildings.

He passed a closed campground on the side of a hill, and found the chain-link fence at the end of the street open. Two men were waiting for him at the foot of the launching crane. Miqui got out of the truck and glanced at the yachts, sailboats, and cruisers that swayed in their moorings. The port was deserted, the brunt of the tramontane was concentrated right there, he could see it and hear it, like the wind awakened the present moment. The tinkling of rigging, the creaking of naked masts, and the grazing of metal cables reached him so clearly that it was as if it were all right beside his ear. He would like to have a boat: offset the kilometers of asphalt with nautical miles; float freely on the weekends in a world made entirely of roadway; go fishing in the winter; speed off to the horizon with an outboard motor in the summer, the nose lifted and some chick sunbathing on the bow—a flesh figurehead. And then dive into the sea; the cruiser would be an island for the two of them, the sea a mattress of water, far from everyone, and one day they'd sail leisurely to Morocco to see Ahmed. Hey, Ahmed, take a look at this!

He consoled himself, watching the boat he'd come to take away arrive slowly. Beside the registration numbers there was a name in Cyrillic letters. Some fucking Russian was losing his pleasure cruiser. It was being towed by a teenager in a workboat. The boy stopped beneath the travel lift, tied up his vessel, and jumped onto the motorboat. It wasn't small, it had a command bridge for the driver, berths with portholes, and a Spanish flag on the front. The boy led the straps that hung from the crane down under the hull, first on the stern and then on the bow. He jumped on land, and the lift began to hoist. The boat rose out of the water like a large dead fish. The lift operator lowered it slowly, still dripping, onto the truck, fitting it between the tires. Miqui strapped it down. The whole gunwale stuck out, white with a steel railing, and the command bridge was taller than the truck's cab.

"If that Russian bastard ever comes back, he's gonna find the mooring empty or rented to somebody else," said the supervisor. "They just leave them here for me to deal with. I say: take the boat out to sea and dump it there. Nobody wants them anyway. Do you know how much gas these things use per mile? You should see the warehouse in Palamós..."

"Russian mafia," said Miqui. "Sucks."

"The whole housing development back there is full of Russians. It looks like Moscow over there. They make these houses that look like bunkers, so they can't be attacked, they gold-plate the swimming pools; it's filled with plainclothes security guards and chauffeured cars with dark windows. One day something bad is gonna happen. They say that half of the government's family members live there."

Miqui went back through Platja d'Aro with the boat on his truck bed, like a short military parade for those tall buildings facing the sea, standing as if they were reviewing a navy display, a boat with the Spanish flag cutting across the avenue without a crew, marching alone before buildings held up by spines of empty staircases, a ghost boat among ghost windows and balconies, through a ghost town taken over by the wind, a warning to the independentist flag wavers: here the troops will arrive by sea, not like in Vidreres, where they came in planes. He glanced up at the roof of his cab and saw the shotgun, maybe it was sending down good vibes. He had it loaded, screwed up his courage, he mentally drew open the curtain again, and again felt the sun shining through the flammable north wind.

No one in Palamós would mind if he arrived a few hours late, he thought, and girls love these kind of stories—a spic like Cindy wouldn't be able to resist the temptation, she'd be creaming. He could drop off the boat later on. They hadn't firmed up a delivery time, no one would miss him, and if they called, he'd say he got a flat, or make up some other excuse. He exited the highway to Palamós, headed toward Girona, stepped on the gas, and passed Llagostera again on his way to Vidreres—he'd stop in for a coffee at the community social club, he had a surprise for Cindy, a little boat trip.

"Are you nuts?"

"I'll take pictures of you with my phone."

He would have her get on the boat, a girl like her doesn't weigh a thing, he'd have her sit up in the cockpit, in the white pleather pilot seat, and take her for a spin around the fields of the plain—he'd keep an eye out for police cars, but even if one passed they wouldn't think to look in the boat, it's just silly, it's probably not even against the law. He'd sail her along the highway; he'd have her in his pocket, take her through the forest, along the paths, and it would seem like she was sailing through the Amazon. It would all look familiar, and what woman, what girl, if she really was that young, would say no to having her picture taken on a good-looking boat; maybe they'd find a captain's hat in the cabin, he could tell her to put it on for a photo to post on Facebook. Back home in her country they'd envy her, their eyes as wide as saucers—and who's that man? Whose boat is that? Have you seen Cindy? I want to move to Spain!—half an hour in the cockpit like a queen, with her hair blowing in the wind, at the time of the day when the fields have soaked up the morning's warmth.

An outing like a ship procession bearing Our Lady of Mount Carmel, Star of the Sea, Immaculate Cindy, what bliss, for a little while he'd make her forget about her miserable life as an immigrant spic. Then he'd drop her off at work, and come back to pick her up when her shift ended that evening.

"In the summer, I'll take you out to sea. I liked you the minute I saw you yesterday. I'm just like that. I thought: why don't you show Cindy the boat, since you're moving it to another storage spot, it doesn't seem like she's having much fun at work."

He sped up on his way to Vidreres as if the cruiser was pushing the truck. It had been years since he'd pulled something like this. He was old enough now to start doing things he was old enough to know better than to do, he thought. If Ahmed were here, he would've laughed and helped him. They would have been a trio. The world didn't end in the apartment in Sils. He wouldn't end up like his father, that's for damn sure.

He exited the main highway. He saw the tree with the bouquet of flowers again. Something must have happened with the two brothers' energy, he thought, two kids younger than him. Just like they passed on their tires to Isma, maybe they passed on their energy to him. Maybe that was what he felt in his blood, what made him pull back the curtain all the way.

That black spot down the hill was the same little whore from the day before. There was no way he was going to pay for sex two days in a row, especially not with Cindy in his sights. But it wasn't even one yet; he had time for a courtesy stop. It was worth it. That girl wouldn't be around for long.

He downshifted and took a good look at her. The looking was always better than the touching, but that little body of hers had the gravity of twenty planets put together. She recognized him from a distance. She stood still, waiting for him, puzzled by what he carried on his flatbed. A boat in Vidreres, what a sight. He downshifted so she could get an eyeful. The girl put her hands on her hips again. What do you think, my love, of what I brought for you? Should we hop on board and skip town? Go east, to your country? Would you get onboard, hmm? We'll go to the beach; I'll untie the boat, reverse on the sand, sink the truck in the water... fuck this truck, it's a clunker, we're not coming back anyway, the boat floats, we'll climb on, see ya on the flip side... He smiled and glanced in the mirror. Behind him the highway was empty. He braked gradually and stopped the truck right in front of the girl.

She approached him. She walked onto the asphalt, crossed a lane, and drew up close to the truck's window. My god, the way she moved. Such beauty. You had to admit that. Cindy was a piece of shit next to her. She was hotter today than yesterday. Better and better. Let's get married, you ballbuster. How old could she be? She was beyond age. She couldn't be pigeonholed. She was explosive.

He lowered the window all the way down, starting to feel the erection—you'd have to be a robot to resist her, there was no point, it was impossible—she'd give her price, he'd pay it. He swallowed hard, but before asking her what she was charging, he stopped. The chick stared at him, in a way whores never do, almost defiant. Maybe she was high again. It wasn't easy to figure out a chick like that, you had to be really cold-blooded. Maybe she'd fallen in love with him and she'd do it for free.

Suddenly, the girl raised her fist and separated out her middle finger, the same gesture as the day before, this time right in his face. Then she lifted her chin, turned around, and went back to her spot.

"Evil bitch. Who does she think she is?" He stuck his head through the window and said, in Spanish, "Come on. How much? Come on. Twenty? Is twenty OK? All right. Twenty. Come on. Twenty. OK."

The girl shook her head and showed him an open palm.

"Five? Fifty?"

She nodded.

"No fucking way," said Miqui.

Who did she think she was, this piece of shit with curls? Gabriella Fox, Sarah Vandella, Lorena Velásquez? Since when did goddesses of porn do it with truckers in Vidreres? Fucking worthless ignorant whore.

The shotgun was held to the roof of the cab by two hooks. It was easy to pull down. He looked in the rearview mirror and saw no one. The makeshift gun rack worked. He placed the gun on his knees. Now you'll see. Stupid whore wasn't expecting that, she was still laughing when Miqui lifted the shotgun and aimed it at her. She froze. She turned and started to run. Now he was the one laughing. Evil bitch didn't know where to go. She ran like a rabbit, to the right, then the left, then she almost fell. She wouldn't forget this soon.

First lesson, stupid whore: don't fuck with strangers. Don't try someone's patience when you don't know who you're dealing with. Don't be so conceited.

What if he gave her the lesson she deserved? What if he shot her? He undid the safety. You can't just go around provoking people, you piece of shit, one day you'll run into someone with a real nasty streak.

Seriously: he hadn't planned on firing the gun. But things happen. Miqui heard a horn he wasn't expecting, as if a car was about to plow into him. The jolt stiffened his fingers. His index finger pulled the trigger and the shotgun went off. He had never fired a real shotgun. The kickback sent him flying. His heart skipped a beat. He was left stunned and deaf. The cab filled with smoke and he couldn't see anything. He coughed. The horn was still going off, frantically. His shoulder hurt. He looked through the other window and saw the van that kept track of the girl. The man inside was desperately honking the horn. Miqui's heart was going a thousand miles an hour. His fingers and legs trembling, he put the truck into first and stepped on the gas. The wheels spun before gripping the asphalt—they were too worn, fucking Isma. Shit, shit, shit. He got into second gear, into third, and when he reached the first houses of Vidreres, he looked into the rearview mirror.

They hadn't followed him. The whore was running across the highway to the van. The driver opened the door and the girl got in, crouching down inside the van to hide and cry. The van sped down the road, growing smaller as it went toward the main highway.

The streets of Vidreres weren't as deserted as the day before. The truck's engine once again filled them with noise. The women making lunch looked out their kitchen windows—maybe for the second time, maybe they'd looked up before, surprised by the distant thundering of the buckshot—what was that? Hunters, on a Tuesday? Please, not another accident. They were surprised to see the cruiser passing by, a big white plastic shoe, and thought about how it would be carnival soon and that some group must be secretly preparing a parade float with sailors—sailors in Vidreres, that's a good one. Children screamed with excitement when they saw the cruiser pass by on the other side of the schoolyard gate through the school's large windows, and their teacher had to scold them. A motorboat in Vidreres. Passing by the ATO milk packaging plant, passing the bakery and the little supermarket, passing the tobacconist's and the town hall, toward the church, a boat on a flood of invisible water. Vidreres-Venice, such a thing had never been seen. A boat sailing along narrow streets, between the first-floor balconies, over dry fish and mermaids, over submarine cars and seaweed dogs. The trucker already knew where to park, and when he passed in front of the office with the red Santander Bank sign he thought that must have been where the potbellied man from the day before worked. Hadn't he told him not to come back to Vidreres? Well, here he was again. And, to let him know, he honked his horn a couple of times.

He parked and made sure the truck's door was securely closed. He was safeguarding a weapon. He walked toward the community center without thinking any more about the bank, but just as he passed in front of the office the door opened. There was his buddy, with his white shirt and dark tie, looking fatter than the day before, his face redder, a good candidate for a heart attack. And he had the balls to come out and point at him. Today, everybody and their mother was skating on thin ice.

"Where are you going?"

He answered with a contemptuous smile. The door opened again and another man came out, about the same age and wearing the same uniform, but thinner.

"What's wrong, Ernest?"

"Nothing," said Ernest. "Somebody I know."

"Who is he?"

Miqui didn't stop. Who was that shitty banker anyway? Cindy's father? Her chaperone? Her protector? He didn't even turn to provoke him. He went into the club with a generous smile, with the energy he'd released inside himself by pulling that trigger: his prize for having successfully taken a risk. He could have killed her and he hadn't.

He found it odd to see people sitting around the tables inside the club, with its normal atmosphere, the same dark interior it must have had when it opened its doors a hundred years ago, the ceiling so high you assumed there were cobwebs, the checkered floor with white squares already graying and black ones fading, and the occasional chipped corner of a tile, some split in two, others ill-fitting. More than one club member took their eyes off the television newscaster to look at Miqui. There was a novelty inside the club now, a stranger who had just come in at noon, that intimate time of the day. None of this should've surprised him. When someone from out of town walked into the bar in the Sils town square they got the same welcome. Social clubs were the engines that moved the towns—there were others: the town hall, the church, the sports center, the library, and the schools served that same function for the children and teenagers. The folks from Vidreres sat with their own kind, and every table was a toothed gear in a powerful, lubricated motor, and Miqui was a grain of sand that they'd grind, but he saw Cindy at the bar, and her gaze stopped on him. Cindy wasn't part of the machinery either, she couldn't be, with that name; all it took was one look at her, with her thin, straight black hair pulled into a ponytail, her dark skin, her short, indigenous body type, the singsongy South American accent that she'd never be rid of. Miqui sat at the bar, and she was drawn to him like a magnet; of course, he was her savior.

"I'll have a beer."

The waitress smiled and kneeled to get a bottle. She took off the cap and a bit of foam came out. She dried off her fingers, grabbed a mug, and poured the beer into it.

"Were you able to unload, yesterday?"

"I unloaded, now I've come to load up again."

"To load up what?"

"You."

"Me?" She smiled again.

"When do you get off? I want to show you something."

"I'm here until nine, and after that they're expecting me at home."

"Until nine? Don't you need to have lunch? You eat here, too? What is this, the Middle Ages?"

The girl lowered her gaze and shook her head.

It wasn't possible that she ate lunch at the club. She was lying to him. And she had made it clear they wouldn't see each other after work either. She hadn't given any excuse; she hadn't said she was sorry about it. Then Miqui noticed the little man by the register. A short, badly-shaven guy around sixty who turned his back when he saw Miqui looking at him. Fucking old bastard, he must be screwing Cindy. That's why she was so nice and sweet yesterday: the boss wasn't around, he was at the funeral like everyone, except her. Miqui slugged down the rest of his beer and glanced around the place again. Folks from Vidreres having an aperitif and some olives or potato chips. All in the know about when the girl behind the bar had arrived, and why. He could imagine the jokes at first, jokes between men. The owner of the hardware store in Sils, a lifelong bachelor, had a girlfriend from Eastern Europe behind the counter too, blonde and sturdy with green eyes. She didn't even speak Spanish, but waited on you just fine, and it was a pleasure to shop there, because the blonde belonged to all the men in town, in a way. It must have been the same thing with Cindy: these girls had infiltrated like parasites, you saw them everywhere if you looked, the ones who hadn't left despite the recession, wearing rings more effective than wedding bands, invisible rings that everyone knew about.

Cindy's boss looked at her out of the corner of his eye, he was controlling her like that pimp in the van. What a letdown, after I dragged the boat all the way here. First the little whore and now this one. It wasn't his day. Then the banker came into the club and sat down at a table near the door.

What should I do? Wait for him to leave? How long will that take? Can the banker risk coming home late again—what is he thinking? What does he want? To scare me? Provoke me? Please. I can't even be bothered. He greeted him with a nod of the head. He ordered another beer. Patience. Fucking

Cindy. Who does that banker think he is? Who does he think he's messing with? He lifted his beer mug slightly, as if toasting him. It had been a good idea, the day before, taking that idiot for lunch. He couldn't afford what Marga and Cloe charged, and they didn't want to work alone—either you hired them both or you brought someone with you. The idiot paid for both of them. What a loser. What do you want, for this to come to blows outside, with that potbelly? Should we meet up at the tree, now that I've cleared the whores away? Should I show you what I've got in the truck? You could use a little exercise. It cleans you out from the inside. It's not in your best interest to report me. You'd be watching your back for a long time.

But there was someone else in the club. He saw her in a corner, almost hidden. Was the town so small that everyone gathered here? The daughter from the house where he had unloaded his truck the day before—the grieving widow... He might have left without noticing her, if it weren't for the fact that his eyes were automatically drawn to wherever there was a girl; even before seeing her, oh, yeah, she was already out of her black clothes but her skin was still milky white, she was sitting with a boy her own age, a really weird-looking guy, with two ponytails and a ring in his ear, not hanging from it but *inside* the earlobe. They were having a couple of beers; she had dark bags under her eyes from crying, perhaps all night long, the grief she carried was printed on the skin beneath her eyes, but she was already at the club with another guy. Her father—the man who had gone into the house and quickly come back out in different clothes to help him unload the bales; a strong man, a farmer, coming from the funeral of his future son-in-law as if it were the most normal thing in the world, or maybe even relieved to have gotten rid of the suitor who was stealing away his daughter; a man who rolled up his sleeves and got down to work: let's not waste time, let's get this unloaded, and you, girl, tomorrow start fresh, no use crying over something that can't be helped—and her mother must have said: go out, distract yourself, so the girl was already back to normal life, already had a friend consoling her. If they were out like that, so soon after, it meant they were friends. She hadn't been waiting for her fiancé to die so she could move to the next one on the list. No, she was still single. Helpless and in free fall, waiting for someone to put out their arms and save her.

He ordered a third beer. His vision improved with a hint of alcohol in his blood, like glasses that sharpened reality, making his visual impressions slightly tactile. A strong tramontane inside him. The girl's dress fit her body so well. She wasn't exactly a model, he had to admit, but she still exuded the same desolation she'd had when he'd seen her yesterday, a morbid attractiveness, a helplessness that made her passivity irresistible. Because that was what made a woman: passivity, the very earth from which men spring. They were amphorae, maternal vessels, it wasn't their fault, it was their nature. He had taped up a photo of a porn star next to the stereo in the truck; he chose it with Ahmed on a public computer at a roadside bar—the Virgin Mary, that was what Ahmed called her—truckers keep photos like that, all with the same puffy lips and bell-shaped breasts, amulets of fertility, an antidote to the CD of love songs. Sometimes, Miqui accepted that this obsession—his schlong growing like a snake under tables, sniffing around, searching on its own, without him—was an attempt to find the river in which to let himself be carried off on the current of a relationship that would make him lose sight of the world. That happened to everyone, didn't it? So, if he was looking for a girlfriend, someone to disappear into, was this flitting from one to the next just because he hadn't found a woman ample enough to take him in whole? Was he that overwhelming?

The checkered floor made him think of a chessboard. Let's play a game: he has Cindy behind the bar, an already captured piece, a bishop retired from the game; he has the old man at the register, the supervisor, a fucking pawn with a nasty face that could turn into a queen by calling the police or kicking him out of the place if things got rowdy with the banker; he has the banker, a castle controlling one corner of the board near the door, with little room for movement, who doesn't want him to go near the girl at the bar, a girl who Miqui was no longer the least bit interested in; and, next to another puny pawn—the bootlicker who happens to be buying her drinks at the moment, the freak with the perforated ear—there is the piece he wants, the piece that rules over the playing board, his white queen.

He would approach her in two moves. First, he would go to the bathroom. That would be the excuse. There he would have a look in the mirror. He was plenty attractive, his work kept him in shape, and it was a pleasure to have the mirror remind him of that. On the way out he would walk past her table.

The checkered floor continued inside the bathroom. There was no one in there. Half a dozen urinals on the wall, whose white tiles came together in moldy stripes. Bits of blue soap on the urinals' screens. The door opened again and closed behind him. He saw the bank clerk's red boots in the mirror.

"Tell me something," said the banker as he opened the tap and dampened his inflamed face. "Are you trying to provoke me?"

"Relax, I'm not here because of you. But tell me something. Were you born yesterday, or are you the only one in Vidreres who doesn't know why that girl works here?"

"I already told you I'm not from Vidreres. If I were twenty years younger, I'd tell it to you in a different way."

"I bet you would. What's wrong, you didn't have a good time yesterday? Isn't Marga hot? Did she do that bit with the wings?"

"Has anyone ever told you that you're crazy?"

The banker turned tail and fled the bathroom. He had performed. He could rest easy now, go home to his wife and kids, wherever they were. He had assuaged his conscience. Miqui splashed a little water on his hair, smoothed it out. He gave the banker a few seconds to leave the club, to save himself from having to see him again.

He left the bathroom and went straight over to the girl's table, following the diagonal line of black tiles to the table. The couple was very attentively looking at the screen of a cell phone the young man held in his hand. They had brought their chairs closer together and were both watching something. It didn't seem like something funny exactly, but it did seem very interesting. They were quiet. Photographs of the dead guy, probably. The day right after the funeral? She didn't lift her head and Miqui had to slow down. He pretended to be looking at his watch. The young man was doing something with the phone as he stepped in front of her. Finally, she looked up.

"Excuse me," said Miqui. "I saw you, and I just wanted to say that I'm so sorry."

"Who are you?"

"Oh . . . I'm Miquel, Miqui, I was at your house yesterday, I came with my truck to bring seventy-five bales, you must not have even seen me. I'm very sorry. I saw you and I wanted to say. . . I'm so sorry. That's all."

She gave a polite half-smile. If she stood up, Miqui had won the game. Maybe she wouldn't get up. The weird guy next to her was waiting. Miqui imagined her in Cindy's place, on the cruiser. He imagined her sailing with him. In a bikini. That white skin getting toasted. Tan, hot. But no. Don't even think it. It wouldn't work with her. She was older than Cindy. And he had seen her house, surrounded by fields, with animals and tractors, with dogs and horses. Those people were loaded. If they didn't have a mooring in Port d'Aro it was because they didn't want one. A cruiser? Why are you even telling me this? We have a yacht. We sail to Majorca. Once we went to the Baltics. Her father had called Miqui *sir*. Not everyone was a sand jockey like Ahmed or a whore like Goldilocks or a spic like Cindy. There were still normal people around. There were young people with futures. That's where her white coloring came from, from the fat in a healthy diet. She should be feeling sorry for him, a fucking trucker.

Maybe she did. For two seconds she kept her eyes lowered, until she made up her mind. She got up from her chair. A kiss on each cheek and her name.

"Iona." And Miqui finished it in his head: Iona Sureda. Checkmate. Her father had signed the receipt.

"If you ever need a truck…" He handed them each a business card and went back to the bar.

Cindy hadn't missed the scene. She gave him his change for the beers with a furious expression. Miqui sat down with his back to the bar, staring at Iona. He could look her up and down with no problem: they were busy with the cell phone.

There was a large blue anchor painted on the entrance to the warehouse in Palamós. Outside, behind a wall, there was a ship graveyard. You could see it perfectly from the truck, injured boats, faded and dirty from being left out in the elements, with flaking paint, dented metal, broken glass, and amputated pieces that had been used as replacement parts for newer boats. A raspberry patch had slowly invaded one area of the cemetery, the brambles growing and taking over some of the ships, hugging them, tangling around and covering them like a slow green wave, a thorny wave that a bow, a submerged berth, or a bit of railing occasionally peeked through. Here a propeller blade emerged, over there floated a piece of rudder or a faded orange life vest—like a pot filled with weeds. A bit of chain sparkled between some boats, a hull, busted by some underwater slab, revealed a yacht's abdomen, stuffed with green viscera. To one side, a dozen boat trailers were piled up, their iron rusty and their wheels flat.

He drove the truck into the storehouse. They signaled for him to put it beneath a bridge crane. They unloaded the cruiser, placed it on a forklift, and stored it in a niche of the large metal shelving unit among other boats. Light traveled down to the warehouse floor from some big blue windows near the ceiling. The sun's rays reached the ground, falling on the sunken fleet, intact shipwrecks in the belly of the Palamós storehouse, gathered from sport marinas all up and down the Costa Brava: yachts, outboard boats, pleasure cruisers, sailboats, and catamarans resting on the shelves like a collection of defeated trophies. The sailboats had no masts, and they'd taken the motors out of the ships, lining them up against a wall. There were boats like his, motorboats in all sizes, shapes, and colors. You could look up at the higher ones, they had names like Grace, Sirenamar, Lola, and Xaloc. If he had any savings, he probably could have bought one cheap, their original owners must already have boats twice as long on the other side of the planet.

Returning to Sils, he left the road and drove the truck into a forest at the foot of the Gavarres mountains to dump the tires. The sharp north wind was stripping the trees of their leaves. It had rained recently, but he wasn't worried about the puddles on the road, the Atego's weight allowed him to go anywhere. The low branches of the holm oaks and pine trees grazed the top of the cab, and the forest gradually swallowed it up, as if it were a submarine. He followed the dirt road until he reached a clearing where it would be easy to maneuver the truck around.

He turned off the engine and remained in the cab, watching how the north wind moved the branches, making them seem somewhat hysterical. The birds came to rest in the trees. He lowered the window. He pulled down the shotgun, rested its barrel on the glass, and took aim at a sparrow perched in a pine. There was one cartridge left in the chamber. The sparrow flew off. He followed it with the barrel. He had to practice a lot if he wanted to be a good shot. What would have happened if he'd killed that little whore? Nothing. The pimp in the van wouldn't have wanted any problems. He would have just left it at that. Miqui would have gone straight to Palamós to drop off the boat. He would be right where he was. But he wouldn't know the name of the widow.

"Has anyone ever told you that you're crazy?"

But being crazy means that you don't know it. How could you be crazy and know it? True lunatics live on a cloud. Maybe he was cold and analytical sometimes. Maybe he was a little antisocial, like Isma said, a little bit of a psychopath. But he couldn't know that either. No one could know that.

He shot a tree trunk. Splinters flew. Some hit his face. Too close.

He got out of the cab and climbed onto the truck bed. He started kicking the tires out. When he'd emptied the bed, he went back to the cab. Opening up the glove compartment, he grabbed a half-dozen shells and reloaded the shotgun. He made columns out of the tires by placing one on top of the other. He raised four black columns the size of a person. He tried to knock them down with one shot. That was the start of his shooting practice.

He locked up the truck in the lumber warehouse, leaving the shotgun inside. His apartment was the same as ever, his father shut in his room and the hypocritical voices of the television escaping from beneath the door. He hadn't had any lunch, and he defrosted a baguette, filled it with what he could find, and went to his room to eat. He was tired from the night before. He stretched out on the bed and fell asleep.

He woke up in the middle of the night, got up without switching on the light, sat at his desk, and turned on the computer. The room looked like the moon. The chats, the conversations, continued as always. They would continue until the end of the world. He was there for a while, following the chatter of stupid jokes and demands for attention. One day he would invent a program that gave all those messages meaning, came up with their statistical average, interpreted them. Who were all those people? Who was typing? Robots? It was endless. Like the wind always going up and down the staircases of the empty buildings in Platja d'Aro, like the cylinder of air inside the piles of tires he'd made in the forest, in which a person could stand. Miqui occasionally pulled back the curtains to let light in. But even when he pulled back the curtains, the chat continued. There was always someone on duty. People who never slept. When Miqui dies, the chat will continue. Because there is still another curtain, and behind that other curtain there is someone else, a glowing body sitting alone in front of a keyboard, in a room, in an apartment way up high in one of those empty buildings in the morning, glowing like the screen, and giving off light, a scant light that can't be seen during the day, but you might notice among the audience at the movies or in a theater, or at night if you found it far from the streetlights, walking past you in a dark alley, or in a cave, or in a forest, or if it sat among the passengers on a plane flying at night that had turned off its lights for a moment as it went through some turbulence, when everything was dark in the middle of the night and through the windows you only saw the intermittent beat of the navigation lights on the wings, and beneath the plane the large cushion of clouds illuminated by the moon and, inside the plane, among the passengers lurching as if they were traveling by horse and buggy, that body—neither man nor woman—with its faintly glowing aura, over the laptop, typing. When a train went through a tunnel and for whatever reason the lights didn't work, then you could make it out, always typing, with the screen lit up like a rectangular extension of its skin, a skin through which its inner light passed—the light didn't come from its skeleton or from some phosphorescent blood in its veins, you couldn't see it in an X-ray or in the illumined tree of a circulatory system, it was more like light that swaddled its skin, muscles, veins, and bones, entering and exiting the skin, a light that was both inside and outside that body that typed behind the second curtain, in some apartment in an empty building, and who wasn't human but wasn't a robot either—much less any sort of divine presence or supernatural being—but just an extraterrestrial. And sometimes he saw its silhouette, sometimes it got so close to the curtain that its light came through it, and other times he heard it typing, which was what kept it lit up, so that the humans would receive messages, so that the humans had someone to keep them company, so that they could have a consciousness.

He opened a window next to the chat. He typed "Iona Sureda Vidreres Facebook" into Google. Hundreds of photos to look at. A lot more than he was expecting. Date of birth: 1992. Twenty-one years old, or recently twenty-two. Her and her world, as a child with her parents in their house in Vidreres, with another girl who must have been her sister, and at a certain point a boy, taller than her, appeared, happy and full of life, sticking his head out of a black Peugeot and waving, and Miqui thought that maybe the boy's face would be of use to him, that maybe it was worth downloading the photographs he liked before Iona took them down and there was no trace of them left on the web. He downloaded a dozen and saved them in a folder, and spent a long time looking at photographs of her friends and schoolmates from college, photos of trips to Rome and Amsterdam with her girlfriends, photos of her with animals, with horses, dogs, cats, and the photographs of a girl with her boyfriend. Finally, he wrote a short message to Iona, which he left like bait on the hook— "I really enjoyed meeting you"—to see if he'd be lucky and she'd nibble, and then he went back into the chat, ready for another long night.

BURIED DOGS

I

The telephone rang at seven in the morning, but Iona's mother let her sleep. Around nine, since she hadn't woken up on her own, her mother knocked gently on the door to her room. She went in without turning on the light, sat on the bed, and asked her daughter for a hug. She held her in her arms until Iona started to cry.

"Jaume and Xavi had an accident."

Iona counted the seconds that passed without her mother saying anything more. She waited ten more seconds and then counted to twenty in her head. She bit her tongue—"both of them?"—took in a deep breath and, to put an end to the suffering, said: "Yes."

It had to be a lie. She separated herself from her mother's arms and turned on the light. What nonsense. Things like this don't happen. It's like the lottery: no one's ever won it. It might happen to you, maybe in the future, but never right now, in the present. Perhaps in another life. It's too unreal. She relaxed her head onto the pillow. She settled into her denial. Negating Jaume's death was her way of accepting it. It lifted a weight off her that had threatened to crush her. Jaume wasn't dead, her boyfriend since high school hadn't died in an accident, it couldn't be. On Friday he had picked her up in his car in Bellaterra; they went to Barcelona to check prices at the travel agencies, and reserved sale tickets for a flight to India that summer. They had those tickets. They had a lot of things to discuss, about the trip and about everything, there were thousands of loose ends to tie up, essential things. If death could be this sudden, then the world would have already stopped spinning—the world was cruel and unfair, but not so precarious. The world is warped, it tends to conspire and get in the way of surprises. Jaume wasn't dead, it had to be someone else, and therefore Jaume was dead. As dead as it was comforting to deny it, and denying it was very comforting, so comforting it was scary.

Iona's mother didn't feel it as intensely. She couldn't deny it with the same ease. That was why she was whimpering, poor thing, she couldn't stifle her sobs. She had burned through the first phase of grief without realizing it and couldn't imagine how alone he had left Iona, with a void beneath her feet: stopped on the bridge dangling between before and after, clinging to denial until she can get out of herself, go find Jaume, go to the last time she'd seen him, twenty-four hours earlier, when he told her:

"I have to go with Xavi to the concert. I owe it to him, he's my brother, we always help each other out. Come with us if you want."

He would have taken her by the hand and led her like a lamb to the slaughter. He already knew the path, she just had to go with him. Along the way they would embrace. If there was nothing to be done, it was all the same. What did it matter. Everything converged and became one. She would meld with him before he left. He would take Iona with him, Iona with her terrifying comfort.

Meanwhile, she would wait for reality to show up. Everyone erects barriers against the evils of the world. We all expect death every day without despairing. If nothing can be done, there's no point in even thinking about it. Someone who's on death row or terminally ill suffers because they've compressed death into the few hours they have left of life. Meanwhile, others live with a death that is a drop of poison diluted in the sea, an invisible mine that floats, adrift. That was how Iona planned to wait for Jaume's death—until reality came to impose itself on her denial.

To prepare a defense—to try and maintain the denial, ideally until the moment of her own death—she considered her experiences. What training could she count on? She needed every resource. Not even her mother had lived through a trauma like the one she was up against. A girl from the city, from Girona or Barcelona, would make an appointment with a psychologist. In Vidreres, because of the way Vidreres was, she would have to deal with it herself. How long could her denial hold out, accepting Jaume's death by negating it, in that effective but shaky balance? Tragedies like hers were kept hidden, she wasn't aware of any other case; she'd be starting from zero, and would have to take advantage of every second—the first moments were precious if she wanted a solid foundation.

She made a list of defensive materials. An inventory

of experiences. To start with, she had the death of three grandparents when she was a girl: three expected deaths, old people who lost their appetite for living and shrank like sick dogs at death's door without making a scene out of it. She knew that the one grandparent she hadn't met was a woman who, in 1957, when her son was a year old, fell into the house well when she went to fill up a bucket. That was why they'd bricked it up. When her grandfather Enric was alive he told the story every once in a while to warn his grandkids of unexpected dangers. When she least expected it, Jaume was swimming at the bottom of the well.

After her grandparents, over the course of a couple of years, Iona experienced the deaths of three of Can Bou's five dogs.

Iona was studying veterinary science. Like many of her classmates, she had chosen the field out of a female altruism that had little to do with the heroic extremes of boys who studied to be oncologists or surgeons, the same altruism that led some of her girlfriends—with old or ill people at home instead of dogs and horses—to study nursing. So a certain percentage of the department was farm girls, future farm vets who were more interested in treating hooved animals than working in a clinic with pet dogs that lived in apartments. In her case, it was yet to be determined. For the moment, she was taking the required classes, Animal Biology, Nervous System Structure and Function, Surgery, Anesthesiology.

So she was used to surgical videos and dissecting animals in the lab, but those experiences weren't of much use to her when—during her second year of study, as part of an intern-ship at the vet's office in Vidreres—she had to administer a lethal injection. She gave the first of thousands of shots she would give to animals being put down over the course of her professional career, if everything went as it should. It was a boxer who entered the office in the arms of an old man from Llagostera. His owner had come there to avoid the shame of bringing his dog to the clinic in his own town. The boxer had grade-6 leishmaniasis, with lesions in its ears and eyes and a bleeding snout; a five-year-old dog that looked fourteen, dry, feverish, and trembling like a leaf; an animal that couldn't stand up and was having so much trouble breathing that it had to cough to keep from choking. The veterinarian put it on the table, and Iona shifted her anguish over the dog to anger at its owner. That irresponsible old man deserved a good chewing out—which he wouldn't get because the poor animal wasn't the customer, he was—for having let the dog get to such a state. He hadn't had the charity to give the dog a measly antibiotic, nor the compassion to give him a painkiller, nothing—cheapness that skimped on money and feelings like they were the same thing. Not even a glance to say good-bye to his dog before abandoning him to his fate. It must have been months, probably years, that the owner had looked away to avoid seeing the illness eating away at his dog, and now he was unable to hold out to the end of its agony.

Watching the old coward leave, Iona suddenly felt a stab of pity. Maybe some sort of competition had arisen between the man and the dog, maybe the old guy was afraid the animal would outlive him. But how was that the dog's fault? And then, who do you choose? The animal or the person? Was she sure that old man deserved a chewing out? The simplicity, the coldness with which we deal with animals, is the same as how doctors and nurses have to treat their patients at the hospital. But in hospitals they don't have to deal with putting people down. Iona wasn't prepared to put Jaume to sleep. The veterinarian passed her the syringe, and she noticed the dog wasn't wearing a tag. She had no way of knowing its name. The owner had already left the operating room, had probably already paid for the visit and the cremation and left. The vet turned his back to her, leaving her alone with the dog with no name. Who could possibly know who Jaume was with now? She stuck the needle through the rubber lid on the glass vial, sucked up the phenobarbital, and looked into the dog's eyes, which had a scabby film. She thought that if the owner had left, she could take the dog home, give him a few last days of analgesics and love. This creature passed through the world knowing so little of the good things it had to offer, overestimating the scraps of affection the old man gave it . . . If only she could at least pet it and say its name . . . Hey, dog. What's your name? But the veterinarian muttered behind her, "Help him, Iona," and she stabbed the needle in deep, so as not to have to think about it any more; she injected the poison, and ten seconds later the dog's heart stopped.

That internship didn't prepare her for the death of her own dogs. Luckily, none of the three had to be put to sleep. The first one died of a tumor, the second was run over, and the third got a virus that was too much for him at his age. As with her three grandparents, the deaths all happened over the course of a few months, as if they were following each other. Iona gave the dogs medication, dressed their wounds, and eased their suffering. Against all logic—and now that frightened her—each death was harder to come to terms with than the one before it, as if pain was cumulative, as if the death of the last dog, whose name was Frare, dragged with it the death of the previous one, Lluna, and the death of Lluna still dragged along the death of Bobi, and, further back in time, Bobi's death dragged with it Grandpa Enric's, and Grandpa Enric's the other three, in a chain that each added death made harder to pull, as if Iona had to physically drag around the corpses. Maybe it was that she didn't want to abandon any of them. Maybe now she'd be forced to let go of the dead weight, maybe she'd have to exchange . . . What? Three dogs? A couple of grandparents? The whole chain, to deal with Jaume?

Each time, Iona learned more about death, which was why each death weighed on her more. She was feeling around in the void, measuring it. Unlike other experiences she'd had, friends, Jaume, college, the shared apartment in Cerdanyola, each new death affected her more. Each death that affected her, that is, because she was also mature enough not to suffer over the deaths of people she barely knew, despite how unfortunate or unpleasant those deaths might be. The death of a stranger, even if it was broadcast live on television—or particularly then—left her indifferent, and she analyzed it with the coldness with which, years later, if everything went the way it should, she would analyze the deaths of tons of dogs and cats, turtles and caged birds if she opened up her own office, or of cows, horses, and pigs if she finally decided to work the farms. But sometimes the death of a stranger—like that first boxer with leishmaniasis—made her guts clench unexpectedly, precisely because it was a stranger:

the presence of the void within the void, people or animals about whom she knew their death and only their death, like when she read in an obituary or on a tombstone the first and last name of someone who only existed because they'd ceased to exist, devoured in the flash of a name.

Unlike her younger sister, Iona didn't miss the burials of any of the three dogs they'd grown up with. She went with her father, the spade, and the bag with the dead dog in it, each time. She wanted to retain the light of their brown and black fur. Person, animal, or landscape—it happened like with the professors at college: learning wasn't merely receiving, it was an exchange. Nothing was free, getting to know someone meant giving part of your life, and that life was what you cried over later, when he took it with him into the void. And right now Jaume was fleeing like a thief.

With each dog's death, the burial ground beneath the cherry tree, the part of Can Bou that was the dog cemetery, grew. Iona would never have asked her father to take the dogs to the incinerator, the way vets do and as she would have to with their two riding horses when the moment came. There was an animal hierarchy; they just threw the dead cats into the garbage. But the farmers wanted their loved ones close, so they did with the dogs what they couldn't, unfortunately, do with their family members and themselves—much less with their friends and fiancés. They bury them at the foot of the cherry tree on the land where they'd been born and had always lived, keep them with them, mix what was taken from them back into their own land.

Her father put the old soil bag that now held the dead

dog down beneath the cherry tree and started to dig, eight or ten paces from the trunk. Iona worried she'd hear a skeleton breaking, the spade's tip cracking a jawbone, the rosary of a spine or a tail, even though her father knew perfectly where he'd buried the last dog and shifted around the tree. He went around the cherry tree creating a spiral of dead dogs, beginning at the base of the trunk itself, as if linking up with the chain of corpses that started with the first Suredas who'd lived at Can Bou and planted the first of all the cherry trees, which would later grow in this same spot, one on top of the other, like a tranquil geyser of wood and leaves. Her parents, grandparents, and great-grandparents had buried the parents, grandparents, and great-grandparents of the dogs that her father was now burying, and the radius and perimeter of the fenceless cemetery grew around the cherry tree.

They dug up more and more earth each time, and everyone who knew where the dog cemetery was—all the Suredas—could tell by the color of the grass how far it extended. The perimeter was greener, more lush; as if the dead dogs were trying to escape from underground, and had only been able to carry their spoils to the edge of the grass. The cemetery extended about ten meters from the trunk; it was already getting close to Can Bou's other cherry tree— and would eventually reach the house itself—yet, even still, Iona worried that her father would break some bone with his spade. They were just bones now, nothing more, fragments of white calcium, but in his daughter's mind they were bits of the vessels that held what the dogs had taken with them, and, if an archeologist ever put them back together, he would no longer be assembling dog skeletons, but rather, jugs, small chests, and cups for the ashes stolen from the living. Each of those three dogs that died after her grandparents' deaths had snatched an increasingly large bit of Iona's life from her, each death hurt her more, each one was a stronger earthquake whose epicenter was the last dog's grave. The trembling, the shaking, the jolts came from the last link in a chain that was choking Iona like a snake around her neck, a spiral that began with three or four dead grandparents and ended with a pack of dogs who ran, crazed by rage and anguish, around the roots of the cherry tree they were tied to, a whirlwind of underground dogs who barked with mouths full of sand, who pursued her, galloping beneath her feet, sticking their open jaws out of the earth like an agave plant and biting her ankles so she could taste death, not abstraction: a precise, clean cut of flesh taken from her person, from her humanity, from all that was contained within the six or seven buried vessels—three or four grandparents, three dogs—alive and dead at the same time. Everything they took from her past, which was also alive and dead at the same time: playing with her grandparents and her dogs, conversations they'd had when she was little, when Iona was a puppy and Frare was a four-year-old girl. They bit her so she would begin to understand what it meant to cease to be oneself, to be devoured, cannibalized by poor Jaume, who would soon join the dogs underground, who came toward her from a distance with his arms emptied of everything he had taken from her, who walked beneath her like her shadow, an image of Iona trembling in the well water.

The deaths of the last two dogs, Lluna and Frare, hurt more than the deaths of all four grandparents put together. It wasn't a question of quantity, but rather of quality. Maybe it's that one suffering has nothing to do with another: pain, when it's so great, just blends together, no matter what the source. Or that was what she liked to think. Was that why she studied veterinary science? To learn to care more about a person's death than an animal's? To prepare herself for Jaume's death? Did her inconsolable grief over Frare's death have anything to do with him being an animal and not a person? People are much more limited, people have that mechanical part, that rational, abstract, imposed part: reason. It's like poison because it pushes life into a corner, adulterates it, separates it from itself. That was how she was managing, right now, to experience her boyfriend's death so happily, so cerebrally; thanks to that she could fool herself with denial that denied on another level, because each level, each superimposed level of awareness, distanced her from the truth of death. Every person—her mother sobbing beside her, wondering if she should keep on sobbing, whether sobbing was really helping her daughter or in fact the opposite—was the separation of a person, death in life; every person would always be incomplete because they couldn't ever reach themselves, at least in this life they couldn't ever catch up to themselves, and it was a question she often asked herself while she was studying for exams or writing a term paper, immersed in the classifications of breeds and species and chemical formulas, a question that she still hadn't found the right way to phrase but was something like: could she ever catch up to the animals that she would cure? Just like when she jammed that needle into the boxer, wasn't she like a god to those animals and, as a god, a defective being, beneath her creation, which she was forced to set free—to believe in—and, therefore, to lose for herself, just like parents lost their children because they remain beneath them, as all creators remain beneath their creations?

She saw it with the experience she was starting to have of the enormous death that was—that over time would become—the death of her beloved, of her future, of someone like her, on her level, of that which she had started to pursue and that was perhaps her herself, Iona herself. Animals, on the other hand, in their purity, live more deeply, closer to the heart of the universe, closer to the heart of life, without the painful, banal distractions people have; they have a pure experience of hate and love, of sex and motherhood, of family and food, of sickness and, above all, death. If only she could have learned more from the death of her three dogs! Animals were ahead of people, in a world without animals man would never understand himself, he wouldn't know how to behave or how to accept his situation. Dogs' loyalty and love for the humans they live with give rise to greater loyalty and love in their owners. First the dog and then the person. She had also seen it with the two horses at Can Bou, one for each sister.

From animals, man learned to settle. What could he possibly figure out for himself, stuck in his lie? Lies can't even exist on their own. Man had to imitate animals in order to be someone and survive. There are no tragedies in nature; there is no expectation of pain. There is a single, authentic pain. Just one, and it is real.

Every death told her: you are dead and that's why you must live. You have to live because you're dead. If you weren't dead, it wouldn't make sense for you to live. But you are dead, and therefore you have to live life and not live death. If you were alive, you'd have to live death. That's why you're dead: live life. But Iona still remained in denial, waiting for the arrival of authentic death.

"You go with your sister tonight and I'll take my brother, okay?"

"Why don't you lend him your car and we'll take mine?"

"Because his is in the shop, he crashed it last night. He drove it into a ravine. He drives like a psycho, and I don't trust him with my things, you know how he is, all he ever thinks about is girls. Look what he did to his car, and you want me to lend him mine, one he's never driven before, so he can kill himself? You want him to drive my car off a cliff? What am I gonna drive then? Yours?"

Poor Xavi. They should have lent it to him. He wouldn't have done worse than his brother.

The morning after that conversation, her mother was weeping in Iona's room, waiting for her daughter to get dressed. It had been more than ten years since Iona had been naked in front of her mother, but she didn't ask her to leave and just swallowed her embarrassment. She was thinking about how provisional denial is; the wave of reality was heading toward her, underground. Soon, the only thing she'd be able to do would be to flee. Until one day she'd wake up and find that it had all been fake. But that might take some time. Her life from now on had to be parenthetical, until the wave of reality flooded the dream of Jaume's death and it turned out that he was alive.

"What should I wear?"

"Wear whatever you were planning to. You don't have to go anywhere. Llúcia asked me not to take you there. They won't open the viewing room until this afternoon."

She pulled off her shirt and presented her body to her mother as if returning a recyclable. The last person who saw her naked was Jaume.

Would her mother have taken off her clothes in front of her? Iona's mother couldn't think that much. She was too sad, she was sobbing, crying; she was surprised by her daughter's impassivity, but Iona couldn't cry with her, she had to think, she had to feed her brain because leaving it alone would be like leaving a hungry baby alone with a plate of poison.

She saw a drop of blood on the sheets. She felt wetness on her inner thigh. Her period had come early to eliminate any doubt. Her body didn't want to deny it. Animals accepted, they went straight to sadness, like her mother. She remembered how sad the dogs had been, their eyes damp and their ears lowered, when Grandpa Enric died, when the other dogs died. The knots were coming loose, the blood dripped down, there was nothing you could do, you didn't even feel it coming. It was the protest, the wave of reality. As a person she could deny it, as an animal she couldn't.

That intensity ate away at her. The blood had written on the sheet: HE LEAVES NO ORPHANS. Her mother stopped mid-sob and hugged the pillow. "Thank God." Her daughter, menstruating, naked, twenty-one years old, her reproductive system at its peak... In college they were studying mammal morphology, animal reproduction and obstetrics, she would find herself one day acting as a midwife to dogs and cats. If everything went as it should, she would help birth foals, calves, and piglets, she would interfere in the privacy of entering life, and then she would intervene in the exit, sometimes of the same animal, because it wasn't unusual for a veterinarian to find herself having to put down an animal she had helped to bring into the world. She would inseminate and she would sterilize. Come here, boy; that's it, now, go on ahead.

But her period had come early, and that would help her in her denial. She wouldn't have to make the decision of whether to have the child or not. Because, with Jaume dead, would she have more reasons to have it, or less? A dead father gave more reasons than a living father to continue the pregnancy. A dead father couldn't talk, so everything had to continue its course. But how could she have done that—have his child—to Jaume? And to which Jaume, if continuing the pregnancy would mean accepting his death? That was also a crack in the denial: who would want a child after revealing life's uncertainty and absurdity with his own death? Really, who would want that world for his child? Would Xavi and Jaume's parents have had children if they'd known they would end up driving into a tree at twenty and twenty-two years old?

Or at thirty? Or forty? At fifty? Sixty, seventy, eighty? How many would you like, ma'am? Well, if I can't live a hundred years, there's no point. Well, I'll settle for twenty-five. What luck, not to have to think about that. No, thirty or so's enough for me, because I know we're part of a chain and are here to perpetuate the species... And what if you don't have kids? What if you can't or you die too soon, like Jaume? Here we can only guarantee you a link to the dead, ma'am.

And what if it wasn't her period? What if it was an early miscarriage? A miscarriage before fertilization, a period coming early to impede a birth, nature rushing to expel the part that came from him, the part he had wasted, and replace it as fast as possible, to give someone else a chance, a better role model for Iona's child. Nature wasn't rushing. Nature was immediate.

Jaume hadn't even been buried, and he'd already lost all his rights. Nature went against itself by bringing you into the world, but when it came back for you it regained its place on the throne. She had gotten naked in front of her mother and, at some point, she would do it in front of another boy. She would let another boy undress her, even if just to reclaim her own body, while she waited for Jaume, so she could give it back to him. Death—that death that wasn't—simplified things. All her doubts about Jaume, all the ambiguities constructed in the four or five years they'd been dating, all the inaccuracies, were gone with his death, as if down the drain. Everything that was unresolved, everything that still had to be discussed.

She covered her thigh with her panties and quickly grabbed some clean ones. She pulled up the top sheet, crumpled it, placed it over the stain, and left the room. She went into the bathroom, washed, and put in a tampon. When she came back to the bedroom, her mother had laid out her clothes on the mattress. She had stripped the sheets off the bed; they were in a pile on the floor. Beside her mother was Mireia, her younger sister.

"I have to get dressed," said Iona.

Her breasts were still showing, her breasts which were

Jaume's and his children's, because they'd wanted to have children. They had talked about it, picked names, names that were now lethal... Her forsaken breasts were now, once again, her's. Not even that. They were shrinking. They were regressing to a barren girl's. My god. Her pubis shaved the way Jaume liked it. How could her mother welcome the part of him that her daughter embodied?

She wanted to tell her sister that everything was okay; as the older one she had to take the lead and guide her little sister, but she couldn't. She hugged her to console her. Her sister was crying for her, but Iona had to bear the denial of Jaume's death alone, and she felt it scattering, she couldn't hold on to the denial; it was slipping through her fingers; it was bringing her other deaths to life, four grandparents, three dogs, so vivid that if the well had been open, she would have asked Mireia to accompany her to see the woman at the bottom, swimming in her clothes, peaceful, trusting, waiting for them to throw her a rope. That woman was Jaume's death. It wasn't going to be easy to settle into living in a false reality. She resisted at the border of fantasy, entering that country had too high a price—insanity—but holding out on the border... it wasn't just that her own body was denying the denial. The denial expanded inside her, a new pregnancy that drove out Jaume's, and countered reality, resituated it, corrected it to underscore the incongruities. Who talked about menstruation? She searched for the cherry tree from the window. It was too sunny for a winter day. No, nothing about menstruation. The cherry tree that festered. The dogs' blood traveled up through its roots, swelling the cherries, dripping off the leaves, trickling down the branches and trunk to the ground and there, in the day's white and intense light, like a frozen flash of lightning, it seemed like the shadow of the fruit tree but wasn't; it was a red shadow, a puddle, the ground was wet. The other cherry tree was also bleeding, and the peach trees had matured so suddenly that the peaches hadn't had time to fall; they had rotted on the branches, and their bone-colored pits hung among the leaves. Late January and that sun. It couldn't be. The pomegranates and figs, filled with seeds, erupted; the apple tree lost its leaves, and its branches curved, loaded down with red apples. The garden covered the tubers' rapes, the pregnant watermelons burst, across the sky came a flock of seagulls from the dump in Solius.

The two sisters and their parents didn't have lunch; they watched television without speaking all afternoon and evening. Then their father said he was going out for a walk through the fields and left. The funeral was the next afternoon. The silence of Can Bou covered the other silences. The televisions' volumes were low, fewer people walked down the streets of town, kids didn't cry. The air had frozen over the plain. Even the weekenders from Barcelona, driving through the fields of Vidreres in search of the freeway, slowed their pace.

"I'm very tired," said Mireia, as the evening drew to a close. "I just want to go to sleep."

"Wait a minute, until your father gets back, and then go on to bed," said her mother. "You don't have to come to the wake."

"I don't think I'll go to the burial either," said Mireia.

Iona felt she should say something, as if she were in charge of protocol and invitations, as if she had the right to excuse her sister from attending. What was the point of her little sister being there? But Jaume and Xavi were dead, and it seemed that, in turn, the two sisters should have to go to the funeral, like an offering to the God who had taken the two brothers and not them. Iona would go as if it were nothing; she would fly over the funeral just as she was flying over this first evening with Jaume dead. The more immediate realities—the furniture in the house, the smells, the words—had intensified, as if to help her hide from what was going on.

"Maybe it's better if you don't come, Mireia," said Iona. "It won't do you any good, not you and not them."

"I'm really sorry, I'm so tired, emotionally. I just don't have the heart, and it's better I say it now. I don't want to worry all night about having to tell you tomorrow. But it seems rude not to go. Wouldn't they have wanted the whole town to see them off? Wouldn't they have come to our funeral, if it had been us?"

"What they would have wanted was to not have the accident. Would you want a funeral full of people?"

"I don't know, Iona."

"Forgive me, Iona," interjected their mother. "Today's not a day for arguing, but the funeral isn't for them; no one expects it to help or to be meaningful to them in any way. The funeral is for those of us left behind, to be there for their parents and to be there for you, to share in the pain."

"Pain can't be shared," said Iona. "And if it could, what would you want, to pass it off on someone else?"

"No, I'd want others to pass it on to me."

"I don't want to pass my pain on to anyone. It's better if Mireia doesn't come."

"And what about Jaume's parents?" said Mireia.

"They'll understand that you're grieving so much you can't go. They won't mind at all. What do we know about their suffering? I don't want a funeral. I want to disappear for everyone in the same moment that everyone disappears for me. I don't want to leave annoying reminders as if I were coming back. I don't even want to leave good memories, no kids, nothing. It's pathetic."

"I'm so sorry. Now I see ..." said Mireia, "that I've been giving it too much importance. It's just a ritual."

"It's a lie, at the worst moment. It's not for the dead; it's for the living, out of fear. The burial isn't to see them off; it's for those who are left behind, like Mom said. To be there for me. To make it clear to me."

"To be there for you and for the four of us, to be together in a difficult moment," said Mireia. "It would be selfish of me not to go."

"So, me not wanting a funeral for myself, is that selfish too?"

"The last thing we want to separate from is people. If you forgo a funeral, that means that you're absolutely positive that everything ends in this world."

"Maybe I just don't want to cling to it desperately. Maybe because I trust that everything doesn't end here."

"But we even bury our animals."

"For the sake of hygiene," said Iona. "No one asks the clinic for their dead animals back. Even here in Vidreres, people call the vet to get rid of a dead dog. I'd rather you didn't come. It's using the dead. We'll parade Xavi and Jaume around, carry them to the church, and have them blessed to make ourselves feel better. There are fifty thousand better places to take them, Mireia. You think Jaume spent much time thinking about God? You think that was on his mind? And what right do we have... But maybe I'm wrong. Maybe it does make sense to take them to the church. To show that they're nothing now, and we can do whatever we want with them. To make it clear who's in charge. It's not important, I don't want you to come if you're tired; in fact, I wish you wouldn't. In fact, I wish you'd decided not to come because you have a party to go to, or something else, something that has nothing to do with Jaume and Xavi."

"Iona..." said their mother.

"I'll go," said Mireia. "I changed my mind."

"Mireia, if you don't want to use them to make yourself feel better, if you want to waive that right, then everyone should understand."

"Your father would be very upset."

"I'm gonna go," said Iona, "but for me it'll be just as if I didn't. I'll be watching it through a pane of glass."

"There is no glass," said her mother.

Her father came in. He had heard the conversation from the entryway. He sat down and said, "Mireia, you will go to the service like everyone else. I went by the funeral home. It's the saddest thing I've ever seen."

Iona thought about Xavi and Jaume's parents, killed by the accident's shock waves. They'd rather forget about her. She would too. She planned to avoid them. As a future daughter-in-law she was dead too. She didn't want to be a zombie daughter-in-law who said "hi" to her zombie in-laws every time she ran into them. Everyone saw them as completely devastated—the way they must see her—but that didn't mean the boys' parents weren't denying the accident. Otherwise, how could they have a wake for them? How could they even breathe? The body is perfidious, but it was also that everyone else was now looking at them through a black filter. But for Jaume and Xavi's parents their two sons weren't dead. They just hadn't heard from them in several hours, they were late coming home, that happened a lot when they went out. And the funeral home and the figures in the coffins? A joke in poor taste. There's plenty of malice in the world.

The living dead lined up at Santa Maria church, slow, pallid, dressed in black, praying. Weeping, mute, secretly violent zombies, making a murmur of moans and sighs between the bare stone walls, sitting on the uncomfortable planks of the pews, coming to pieces, flesh falling, avoiding looking at each other in their embarrassment, and because if they moved, they might lose a leg or an arm, and their heads could roll off their necks and onto the floor. They sat and listened in silence to the mass and would stick it out for all the rest of it, too. They watched the two pale wooden coffins pass between the pews, one with Jaume in it and the other with Xavi, and Iona had the feeling that she was the only living person at the funeral; that only she retained, preserved, and maintained life.

Iona saw Nil Dalmau leaving the church. She had dodged her zombies-in-law, half hiding around a corner, waiting for her parents and her sister to finish what she, because of her privilege as the zombie widow, could shirk. That was when she saw him. It seemed that he was looking for her in the crowd, and was surprised to find her staring at him. She smiled. He was the least strange zombie at the party. The one closest to the world of the living. Everyone should've had to dress as monstrously as him that day—come to the party in costume like clowns to the circus. It had been a while since she'd seen him around town. He hung out with other people, from outside Vidreres, and she'd never seen him with Jaume or Xavi.

She knew him from school, where he was a few grades ahead of her. Later, they'd sent him to private school in Girona. Every once in a long while she'd hear something about what he was up to. She knew he was studying fine arts in Barcelona, or maybe he'd already finished his degree. He was dressed in black from head to toe, he was the blackest of them all, black tie. Outside, he put on a black hat. He wore his hair in two ponytails like an Indian, and had an incipient beard with no moustache. But what turned people's heads, first curious and then repulsed, was his left ear. The lobe looked like the handle of a pitcher. He wore a metal ring inside a large open hole in the earlobe, which was dilated like a tire made of flesh.

If that meant something, Iona wasn't in on it. In the final years of her degree they were studying tropical veterinary science. Recently, iguanas and dragons, snakes, salamanders, chameleons, spiders, and scorpions had become more and more popular; people were tired of the usual four-legged friends. The fad was creatures that were like living fossils, autistic and prelapsarian pets, an incomprehensible world, but, just like those in the know could interpret their friends' terrariums and knew the significance of a certain ophidian,

lepidosauria, or amphibian, every eccentric piece of clothing that boy wore must mean...what? What did it mean?
Everything he'd added over the years to separate himself
from the already somewhat strange little kid she'd known?
And the blue tattoo of a star on the back of his hand? And
the longer fingernails on his pinkies?

They greeted each other with a glance. She avoided him,
but after the burial, at home, while Mireia and their mother
sat in the dining room and their father was helping some
trucker unload bales of hay for the horses, she opened up the
computer and found that Nil Dalmau had started a chat with
her. If she hadn't just seen him, she would have thought his
photograph was a joke.

How are you?

What can I say

Can we talk?

Yeah

How are you?

I don't know

When you know you won't want to talk to me

Probably not

I want to ask you a favor

What

Tonight

What do you want?

To talk to you

Talk now

I want to show you something

What

Some videos

Send them to me

It's dangerous

I can't go out

Yes you can

Not today

Noon tomorrow at the club

II

First thing in the morning on Wednesday, Iona turned on the computer and got a message. "I really enjoyed meeting you." That was the second guy to contact her since the accident. Some loser, at least ten years older than her, some guy she didn't know from Adam, had sent her a message he'd written to himself: I did it, I dangled the bait. Period. Wasn't there an understood grieving period, some buffer from the world to protect her from these little violations?

Because there was Nil Dalmau too; she hadn't seen him in years, and now he resurfaced looking a fright, made a date to meet her at the club, showed her the most unpleasant videos ever, and asked her if they were illegal.

"I would turn you in myself," she'd said, "if I could think past what's happening to me."

She didn't understand anything, and these two guys were helping a lot with that. The world had lost all logic. It was a desert; it had only been three days since the accident, but there was a growing feeling that a war had been lost. Reality plowed ahead, establishing laws that had nothing to do with the ones that'd governed it up until then.

That morning she went back to the university. She left Vidreres after seven, just as the sun was starting to shine, and she saw the tree for the first time since the accident. She knew it was on that road, but avoiding it would have meant a fifteen-kilometer detour to the freeway. She had to face up to that route today, or she wouldn't be able to for a long time. She fixed her eyes straight ahead, through the windshield, and avoided looking at the asphalt to keep from seeing any shards of glass glimmering on the ground or any skid marks. She tried to look at the sky—she didn't want to see a wound on the tree's trunk—but it was no use. They had tied a bouquet to it with the whitest ribbon they could find. She saw the wilted flowers for a moment as short as the one when Jaume had seen that same trunk before slamming into its previous flowerless incarnation. The trunk of his own cherry tree. Who had put the bouquet there? Who had taken the liberty of rubbing the tree in her face, with all its bare branches? Didn't anyone think of her or the boys' parents? Change the road's course, erase it from the map, saw down that plane tree, she didn't want to see the accident every time she passed by.

Hidden, up until then, behind Jaume, Xavi started to make his demands. What about me, Iona? Now you're acting like we don't know each other. Do you think I suffered any less than my brother?

Not even the corpses thought twice before violating her space.

I have something important to tell you, Iona. It was all his fault. I had nothing to do with it. It wouldn't have happened to me. He stole my life, Iona. I was his brother, and he stole everything from me. And all because he didn't want to let me touch his car. How was any of this my fault? I wouldn't have killed him, Iona. I've had accidents, sure, but never bad enough to kill anyone, much less kill my brother. I would have been more careful; I would have been able to regain control of the wheel. I was the younger one, more innocent, we were two years apart; think about what two years means, when you only live to twenty. How could I return to the world now? Who would I trust? Did you notice how they looked at you in the church? Not my parents, my poor parents, they lost two sons, one as a punishment for the other. But you dated Jaume for years. No one was as close to him as you were. You are the heiress, the next in line. Think what he left you. He was driving. It was his fault. Why didn't he lend me the car? He always treated me like a little kid. He had to kill me. Imagine, if he'd just killed himself, the little brother would have ended up growing past the older one. Think about me, Iona. I'm here too. Didn't you see how people were looking at you? He was your boyfriend, Iona; I wasn't the one who was supposed to be by his side on Saturday night. Remember me.

The news had spread through the department, and it was worse than she had expected. All morning her fellow students took advantage of her. It was a practical lesson: How will we treat Iona? How do we treat a client who's just lost her dog? Or a dog that's just lost its owner?

"I just wanted to say that I'm so sorry," said one student, using the exact same words the trucker had the day before.

"Iona, are you okay?" Yes, she's fine, compared to the others.

"Don't worry about not answering my messages, I understand."

Those looks that wanted and taunted.

She didn't think she had the heart to stay in their shared apartment. She went back home, having to drive over that road again, but this time she was prepared. She knew which tree it was, and she was able to save herself from seeing the wound again. She sped up and went right by.

"What's wrong with guys?" she'd asked her sister. "How is it even possible that they're already hitting on me?"

"Don't ask me, you're the one studying veterinary science."

In the midafternoon she went out to take a walk through the fields. Studying was impossible. By the door of the house she found Seda, a mutt who'd shown up at Can Bou a year before with a broken paw, probably from the road. It had been shortly after Frare's death. Iona and her sister cleaned her up, took care of her injury, and gave her a name. Seda had gotten used to lying on the porch; she couldn't keep up with the other dogs because she still limped. It was comforting to find her there, day and night; she had a spot reserved for her under the cherry tree.

The bitch wagged her tail with her ears back, and rubbed up against Iona's legs. When she kneeled down to pet her, they looked into each other's eyes. The eyes of an animal are terrible. Riding a horse you get the impression that the horse's legs are your own, you mentally merge with their gait and become a centaur. But through their eyes you go beyond merging, they are tunnels to a shared world where you can't tell who is what.

A horse neighed softly when it saw Iona was leaving the house without taking the car. She turned around and went past the stables to stroke the horses. Brushing their manes, she saw herself in the well that was the four black balls of their eyes, and then left the building with the dog following her. They went past the two cherry trees, through the gate, and took a dirt road into the fields.

Don't even think about going near town; she didn't want to run in to anyone. The road gently rose and fell again; she could hear the freeway in the distance, but, except for the dog, Iona was quite alone. I wish I could just give in, she thought, kill Jaume right here and now, and lock myself away to cry for fifteen days straight, drop out of school, and change my life. But how could I do that to him?

She took paths that she didn't even take on horseback through the green fields; she followed a dirt trail through the forest to Can Salvi. She crossed under the highway, passed the offices of *El Rec Clar* magazine—the plain was a thin slice of fields—and entered the forest again, following the same path. She knew the way, and went up the hill where, as girls, she and her sister searched for mushrooms with their parents on November Sundays—the only outings they did as a family, right before holing up in the house for winter—and she reached Sant Iscle castle. It was four walls with two circular towers, one of which was reconstructed all the way up to its battlements. They had archeological digs there, last summer they found a children's graveyard, and everyone went to see the skeletons: a dozen skeletons like fish fossils that came from underground; a dozen little skeletons with earth for flesh; the whole mountain, the whole planet was their bodies. She had gone there with Jaume to see the skeletons of the children, medieval skeletons, from before the castle had been built... Why were they buried together, and outside the town? That day she had told Jaume about the cherry tree at Can Bou, expecting him to tell her where their cherry tree was at Can Batlle, or their almond tree, or whatever tree or rock it was. But the question remained: why had they buried those children together, outside of town?

She walked around the castle, which still had its moat; she strolled along its walls with the dog behind her, and at the excavation site she noticed that Seda couldn't go any further, she was limping on her aching, stiff leg. A lame dog, a castle atop a hill with crumpled walls and a view over the whole plain...

She sat down, and Seda stretched out at her feet; she'd made her walk too much, poor thing, she hadn't been thinking about her bum leg. Animals don't complain. She reached down to pet her. Seda brought her snout close and wanted to lick Iona's face, but she didn't even have the strength to get up. Iona gradually calmed her. She thought about the boxer she'd helped die, took Seda's snout between her palms, and stroked her head as if she were that boxer. She looked into her eyes again and said to her:

"It was a second. It was only a second, right? You didn't suffer, it was just a surprise. Like a prick. Because... Where are you? Xavi is with you, isn't he? Tell him not to be mad at me. And not at you, either, you guys are brothers... poor Xavi. We think about him too, he shouldn't worry... If you came back now, it would be like nothing happened. Everyone would act like nothing happened. Really. Your poor parents, you don't know how this is affecting them. If you can leave, you can come back too... I'm convinced of it... If you came back, it wouldn't be any stranger than it is now... and it would be a comfort to everyone... Explain it to Xavi... but, most of all, don't be upset, don't be upset with me, not that... and don't go off on your own, eh, don't leave your brother, stay together, like when you were little, okay? And if you can come back, everything will be the way it was, no one's going to mind at all, don't worry about a thing, really, come back, we'll all be really happy... We have those tickets for the summer... and your parents will be so happy... they're like me, they can't believe it. And my parents will act like nothing happened too. And Mireia. Everyone will. Me too. They'll be so happy, right, Seda? We'll act like nothing happened, right? You don't have to worry about what you did, it wasn't your fault, it wasn't anyone's fault, no one will blame you for anything. All day long I tell myself that you're not dead. But if you are, it doesn't matter... What would it change? Being here a little bit longer? Who cares? What does it matter to anyone? Look around. Remember Nil Dalmau? I saw him yesterday, he wanted to meet up, and I didn't know how to say no; he's the weirdest guy in the world, he has a ring in his ear, *in* his earlobe, he collects insects and... If you were here, he wouldn't have shown them to me. But don't hold it against him, everyone's taking advantage... I guess I should understand, I'm in vet school... I didn't go to class yesterday or the day before; I went back today, Jaume, to see if I'd chosen the wrong profession. Everything's so different now. Do you see poor Seda, how far I made her walk? I wasn't even thinking about her, the poor thing. And now what? How do we get back? But you're okay, right, where you are? Don't be sorry about having to leave... I think you're here and you haven't died, not to me and not to anyone... Isn't he here, Seda? Your leg's hurting, huh?"

She thought about calling her sister to come pick them up in the car, but the path was bad, and Mireia was working in Girona that afternoon anyway. She tried to carry the dog, but Seda got anxious and scratched her, and she wasn't exactly small. She put her down and walked slowly, stopping frequently to give her a chance to catch up. Seda limped behind her. They passed right by the new cemetery and the still-empty morgue, a concrete mass set down between the fields, because the dead no longer fit into the old cemetery, and if the dead didn't fit there, thought Iona, we could bury them like the dogs, at home, beneath the cherry tree, and when the cherry trees died we could take them to the cemetery, bury them stretched out inside the niches. And she thought about how the two brothers were there, on the other side of the wall, beyond the cemetery gates, among the bricks of the niches and among the wood of the coffins, and that she didn't care at all. She could have walked within a meter of their heads or their feet and not have felt a thing, as if they'd been erased, as if they'd never existed.

They were already nearing the house along the back path, and Iona saw her father coming in from the fields with three black day laborers. She rushed over, coming up from behind without them seeing her.

"They were good kids," her father was saying. "They were good kids, but they drove too fast. And better now than later."

Iona couldn't quite catch up with him, Seda was limping more and more. Her father said:

"My daughter will find someone else, it's a tragedy, but you've got to keep going in life, I don't need to tell you guys that, right? You know the boys I'm talking about? Those kids. I'll miss them; no way around that. I would've liked to have a son. But then who'd hire you guys? But that kid wasn't perfect. Where were they coming from, in the wee hours on a Sunday morning? They died coming out of Vidreres. But where were they coming from, at that time of the night? Where were they going? I wonder where all this is going to lead. We won't be able to change Mireia; she'll stay in Girona forever. Real bad luck, shit, you can't even begin to imagine."

"Dad," she said, worried that he would think she'd heard him.

"Oh, there you are. I was just coming to look for you."

Excited by him greeting Iona, the dog trotted as best she could over to her owner. She ran circles around his legs, happy and with her tongue out, but she was in such pain that she wasn't nimble enough and made him stumble. He kicked the dog's belly to get her out of his way, and she cried out, moaned, and lowered her ears as she moved away with her tail between her legs. Ondó, one of the day laborers, was smiling until he saw Iona's expression. Then he looked her in the eye and smiled even wider, revealing all his teeth.

"You mind telling me what's so funny?" she said.

Ondó suddenly stopped smiling. He lowered his gaze and left. There were plenty of people who could work at

Can Bou. These three day laborers shared an apartment in Vidreres with four or five others, and Ondó could ruin it for all of them.

The dog took refuge at Iona's side.

"Why do you let her do that?" her father said. "You're spoiling her, don't they teach you that? What are they teaching you, to give cats manicures?"

Maybe he was right. Maybe they treated animals like humans because they wanted to make them disappear. There was exasperation in her father's face, as if he'd aged five or ten years in the last few days. He was hard to understand on the surface; he was a surly, remote man, and his relationship to the land and the crops made him predictable and simple. You knew there must have been more to him, behind that, and if you were his daughter, you could even rummage through the hidden part, but whatever was there never came to the surface; there were no shadows that hinted at anything more, ever, and so it was as if there was nothing there at all. But the boys' death had touched his depths; he'd known those boys even longer than he'd know Iona, had seen them come into the world, and shared the same skies and seasons with them. More than once they'd come over to Can Bou to lend a hand and, for a man who'd barely had a mother, what had those deaths stirred up? A man who'd had a ghost for a mother must understand what Iona was experiencing. Maybe. Who knew?

"Cals came to see us this morning," said her father, when they hadn't yet entered the house but had already peeled off from the day laborers, who were pedaling toward town. "They're selling the lands of Can Batlle."

Yup. She hadn't counted on the ancestral world, the reality that preceded and survived the dead. Cals with his cane, who you ran into in town every time you went and who showed up at Can Bou two or three times every year since before she'd been born, and who'd be showing up after she was dead. He walked through the fields along the dirt path, came through the gate and into the house to say "hi" as if he were owed something, as if he had every right . . . and who knows, maybe he did. They'd invite him in and offer him a glass of wine. They told him what had happened since his last visit. He shared his information. He stroked the napes of the girls' necks when they were little.

Without the boys, the Batlles couldn't take care of their land. Something lurked behind that fact. How and when did she meet Jaume? They'd gone to school together. They'd started dating in high school. Can Batlle was in the same area, behind the little hill. From Can Bou they could see the two poplars at Can Batlle, one on either side of the big farmhouse. They used to send her over to the Batlles' house for tomato seedlings when she was a little girl. It wasn't unusual to see one or both of the two brothers at Can Bou when they were twelve, thirteen, fourteen years old. In those years they ran through the fields, playing in them, working them, or both. Later, they came over on motorcycle, and, before long, the Sureda sisters each had their own horse and would go riding past Can Batlle. They had occasionally all gone out together, and it seemed meant to be—one brother for each of them.

And while the girls' parents hadn't been pleased when Mireia found work in a shop on Nou Street in Girona, they'd been all smiles when Iona said she wanted to study to become a veterinarian. And while no one but her sister knew anything about Mireia's love life—she'd been dating a boy from Salt for over a year—when Iona started dating Jaume it quickly became common knowledge, not that there was any way they could have hidden it.

The two brothers' deaths had reached the inside of the house; they could be felt beneath the tiles, already settled in their underground rooms.

"Our fields touch each other, over there by the path," her father said, and she hadn't realized, she'd never thought she could have an even more physical relationship with Jaume, but their lands had been touching before they'd even been born.

He would work the land; she would be a vet. No need to open a clinic, no need to leave home.

"Cals filled my head with talk of that land, and he's completely right. If we want it, we have to act fast. Lluís from Can Dalmau wants it too. Before saying anything to your mother, you and I need to talk. To the Batlles, you're not just our daughter. We aren't just any bidder. You have certain rights."

"What do you want? My approval?"

"No. Without the boys, they can't take care of the land. They're not like us, who, over the years, have figured things out. They don't know anything about working with the blacks and North Africans, what a hassle it is. And they're old, and even if they did hire people, what would be the point? They can't take any of it with them. And they don't have family to take over the land. In two months it will all be a jungle. They're in a terrible state. But they won't just sell it to the first bidder who comes along. Cals is totally right about that. You have to come with me. Lluís Dalmau is rich, and he wants the land for his boy."

"Nil Dalmau? Did you see him? Does it look to you like he wants to spend his life..."

"Everybody saw him. That's none of our business. A lot of things happen in life, and Lluís knows that as well as you and I do. Land is land. Isn't Nil older than you? They're not bad folks. They've got a lot of land—the whole Miralles area is theirs. But Can Batlle is here. We've had bad luck, what can I say, but it's just bad luck and nothing more."

The well was in the toolshed, the shed they'd filled on Monday with bales of hay to feed and bed the two horses. Four more dogs emerged to greet the father and daughter. Seda lay in her spot by the door, and Iona sat in a chair waiting for her father.

"It's all set up," her father said, coming out of the house. "We can go over there right now."

The five dogs followed them through the fields. The last one was Seda. It was getting dark. The dogs accompanied them to the end of the path and stopped there. Before turning tail and returning home alone, they sat down for a moment on their haunches, to make sure that the father and daughter were continuing. Iona turned to look at them and was glad for Seda's sake. They sat on the border, as if wanting to convince them to come back.

Can Bou was hidden behind some pine trees. Can Batlle was still far off, but she could see the roof peeking out from behind a small hill, a string of smoke from the chimney, and the tips of the two poplars. Quickly they made their way out of the no-man's-land. It was a relief to walk without speaking. The dogs must already be back at the house. They were barking in the distance, as they always did at dusk. That was when the dogs barked, every day at the same time, it had always been like that; they'd spend fifteen minutes or half an hour yapping at their ghosts, maybe protesting that the blinds were being drawn before the day was over. Their barking grew increasingly faint, and the dogs at Can Batlle took up the slack.

When Iona was about to turn thirteen, her father prepared a surprise for her. He left certain rows unplanted, making a small labyrinth in one of the cornfields. In August, with her birthday approaching, Iona's parents told her she could invite her friends to the labyrinth. The day of the party, at dusk, the same time it was now, they went in with flashlights. The barking of the dogs was the same, though they were different dogs—Frare, Lluna, and Bobi were still alive. Between cousins and friends there must have been a dozen kids; Jaume and Xavier were there too, fourteen and twelve years old then. They ran with their flashlights through the green leaves and unkempt shadows of the ears. Everything smelled of earth, of the cornstalks and sharp leaves that her father had watered that afternoon, of the dry stubble of the surrounding wheat fields. Ears of corn, narrow rows, the crunching of dry leaves beneath their feet, stalks like bones two meters tall—you couldn't see a thing even if you jumped, not the highway, not a single light in any house, just the half moon in the sky. She got separated from Mireia and found herself alone in the labyrinth. She began to worry she'd come across animals in the rows: nocturnal snakes or foxes, as lost as she was, who might follow her or be lying in wait among the stalks; rabid dogs; runaway horses whose running widened the narrow rows, she could hear the gallop; or a bunch of boars who crunched dry leaves beneath their feet and would come charging at her; or ghost children; or a glowing alien among the dark stalks. She stopped and held her breath. She realized that a cage doesn't have to be locked. The dry leaves on the ground shone like tinfoil. She could only hear crickets. The fear wasn't entirely unpleasant, and she had a thought that made her brave, and which would always be with her in moments of fear: that the worst thing that could happen was dying. You could die, but that was the worst that could happen to you.

Now that had changed. It wasn't so clear anymore. Maybe it was worse when someone else died.

They were singing happy birthday. They had started suddenly. She saw a dim light around a corner of the labyrinth, the shadows trembling like her; she ran toward it, and there was Mireia with all the other kids and some parents too, and a cake topped with thirteen candles.

Father and daughter walked through the fields that had been abandoned since Saturday and discovered, here and there, the first signs of neglect: a tool out of place, a sack that should have been picked up, a weed growing on the path to the vegetable garden.

Night would fall before they returned home. They could smell the smoke of burning holm oak wood. There were two cars parked on the threshing floor, one was Xavi's, newly repaired, which would have to be sold too. The dogs knew them and barked more in greeting than in warning. Mateu opened the door for them, and they went into the dining room. The television was on, and a small fire burned in the fireplace with more heat than flame, adding to the oppressive temperature coming from the radiators. Next to the television was a collection of family photographs. The living and the dead from different periods gathered in small, upstanding silver frames—a cemetery crowded with tombstones. There were photographs in black and white and in faded color: weddings, baptisms, vacations, holiday meals; all the subjects were smiling.

Llúcia sat beside the fireplace. She tried to smile at Iona but didn't get up. She kept watching the television show. She and her husband were dressed in black. How long was the grieving period for parents who had lost two sons? That is, if it ever ended, or if they'd even begun, if they'd ever get past the denial. Because they could dress in black, they could go to the funeral and to a thousand masses, sign all the documents and death certificates, cry for weeks and years and decades, and fill the new cemetery with flowers . . . they could both commit suicide one day without ever having given up even an ounce of denial. Because, deep down, they would keep that ace up their sleeve forever.

"I'm so sorry to disturb you, but I think it's best this way," Iona's father said. "Our great-grandparents were neighbors, and maybe even their great-grandparents as well. There are things that have to be said face-to-face. I guess that coming with Iona says enough. Cals says that you're in negotiations with Lluís Dalmau. I want to make it clear that we are interested."

It wasn't just the land he was asking for, but his own daughter. Her mother had recovered her body, her father would recover the land—the land wouldn't die when she died. Iona saw a flash of herself buried beside Jaume, between the two brothers, at the castle's excavation site. Unless something really changed for her sister, it would be Iona's husband who would end up working these fields. She was being given up for adoption to Can Batlle.

"We've spoken with Lluís. He called. We don't even have any nieces or nephews. Llúcia is an only child and my brother is unmarried. I understand what you're asking me. But I can't just give it to you either."

"No one said anything about giving."

"And not the house, as long as we're alive."

My God, thought Iona.

"Now think it over," said her father, as if he were the one giving them something. "And I'll come see you tomorrow at this same time, by myself. You more or less have an idea..."

Iona kept running her gaze over the photographs beside the television. She ordered them by date in her mind, there were about twenty. The oldest ones looked like drawings. A farm couple. Some kids on Palm Sunday. A ninety-year-old man, still working the land. Jaume's grandfather. Jaume's father with a fifty-year-old tractor. Babies. Jaume and Xavi dressed for their communions. The two brothers on their motorcycle from the period when she and Jaume started dating. The two brothers with new cars. They were children. She still perfectly remembered that tee shirt and those pants.

Few parents manage to see the entire lives of their children. She knew the photographs from all the times she'd been in the dining room of that house, but now she was starting to feel the same strangeness with Jaume and Xavi as she'd been feeling with their parents. She saw herself trapped in another life, because she saw that she was in one of the photos too. How was it possible that she'd never noticed it before? Hadn't they shown it to her? Had they put it out recently? It was from Jaume's saint's day, in the summer, half a year ago, after Sunday lunch. Jaume and Xavi were sitting with her at the table in that very dining room where they were now. Iona wanted out from behind that glass, she felt instinctive repulsion, as if she were sitting at the table with two corpses. She grabbed the frame. She wanted to throw it into the fire.

Jaume's mother stood up and took it from her fingers.

"I wanted to ask you for that photograph," said Iona, but Llúcia placed it back down among the other portraits.

"It's very sad for a son to see his mother die. But for a mother to see her son's death . . . two sons' deaths . . ." And she hugged her husband. She had been thinking about it every minute, been waiting for days to get the courage to say those words. How could she accept her survival? How could a mother not feel guilty, a mother who'd brought two sons into the world and let them leave it all alone?

Iona had the instinct to embrace her, but she felt the same repulsion as she felt for the image of the two dead boys in which she appeared. The woman who should have been her second mother was with them, wherever they were, more than here with her. She was in the fire, inside the fireplace, being consumed with her sons, going straight toward death. It pained Iona, but she was unable to approach her;

she would have gotten burned.

When they were about to leave, Iona grabbed the picture again.

"Thank you," she said.

But Llúcia shook her head, no.

"You can't have it, Iona."

"I'm in it."

"Put it back where it was, please."

"It's me, here in the middle, Llúcia. You see that, right? That's me. It's mine." And she headed toward the door. "Good night."

Her father caught up with her on the threshing floor outside.

After dinner, in her room, Iona cut herself out of the photograph. Then she stretched out on the bed with her laptop and reread the message from the trucker. She looked at the photographs she had of Jaume and started erasing them from the folders.

When everyone was in bed, she slipped secretly out of the house. The two horses poked their heads out the stable window. Seda was awake and followed Iona to the cherry tree. Right past where they'd buried Frare, with the same scissors she'd used to cut up the photograph, she opened a small hole in the ground and buried the picture of Jaume and his brother. She had to do it twice because the first time, as soon as she turned around to go back, Seda started scratching at it. She whimpered, it was hurting her injured leg, but she couldn't stop. The second time, Iona stamped down hard on the dirt, took Seda by the collar, and dragged her to the house. One horse snorted, and the other whinnied a little when they saw her returning.

The next day she left early for the university. She glanced at the cherry tree from her car. The bitch had not gone back. It was very foggy. Behind the cherry tree, the giant barrow of the Montseny could barely be seen.

A GREAT PLAIN THAT WAS ALL FIRE AND DEMONS

I

At Can Bou they locked the gate at night, but it was low, and the dogs jumped over it.

Nil got there around three, and turned off the engine and headlights of his car. Everything went well. The dogs came rushing out of the shed, barking, but halfway to him they were silenced by the overwhelming scent. He had the window lowered so they would smell the meat, and he had a rag, wet with urine, tied to the handle on the outside of the door.

He had spent the afternoon at the dog pound in Tossa, chatting with the supervisor and giving water to a dalmatian in heat. He knew the guy—he knew the supervisors at half a dozen dog pounds—and the guy remembered him, because everybody remembered him.

"Where's Ringo?" asked the supervisor.

"Son of a bitch leaves my car covered in hair," answered Nil, as he dried the puddle of piss on the cage's cement floor with the rag. Then the supervisor held the dalmatian while Nil ran the dry tip of the rag along the bitch's ass.

"You could take her with you," said the guy.

"I'll think about it."

"Artists."

People who complicate their lives.

He drove to Can Bou with protective pads on his legs and arms, and gloves so thick he had trouble shifting gears. He carried an open sack on his lap, beneath the steering wheel, wet with blood, with fifteen or twenty kilos of lamb meat that he had deboned himself. He emptied the bag out the window. The dogs jumped the fence and leaped on the meat.

He should have scattered the cuts when he'd thrown them. Now he'd have trouble catching a single dog. They were growling with pleasure, the males hankering to sniff the rag on the door. He grabbed the net from the back seat and went out the passenger side door. He placed a gloved hand on the back of one dog to separate it from the others, but the dog turned its head, bared its teeth, and sank its muzzle into the meat again; they were crazy for the meat.

Then he heard some whimpering from the other side of the gate. A dog was trying to leap over it, but one of its legs kept giving out. He didn't think twice, threw the net on it, climbed the fence, finished wrapping up the animal, and tossed it back over the gate. The bundle fell like dead weight on the other side. He carried it to the trunk, pulled off his leg protection and the gloves, got back in the car through the passenger side, and turned on the engine. Can Bou was still dark.

One of the nice things about spending time at the workmen's shack was being able to watch, every morning, from his fishbowl amid the fields—as he breakfasted behind insulated windows with the heat on—how the fog dispersed and the outlines became sharper. The fields took on depth, the edges of the tree plantations came into focus, and the homes at the center of Vidreres appeared one by one, piled up around Santa Maria, all beneath the bell tower and the church's gabled roof.

The bitch spent the night moaning, and Nil had barely gotten any sleep, but it was still too early to go out for his daily walk around Lake Sils. The fields were wet with dew, and everything was glazed with fog. It seemed that, overnight, without a word, the lake's water had risen up and now again filled the land it had occupied before it'd been drained. Nil had seen photographs of old maps where the lake was larger than the one in Banyoles, and the fog and the dew made him think of the water reemerging from its nocturnal lair, retaking La Selva plain, soaking the lands and turning them into a swamp that grew into a deep lake between the mountain walls of Les Gavarres, Les Guilleries, and L'Ardenya.

The sun came up, the water receded, and all that was left on the entire plain was the shallow pool of Lake Sils. The intermittent streams, the irrigation channels, and the holes in the springs drained the water; the earth sucked it up. While the water on the bottom collected in aquifers, the water on top evaporated and gathered as cloud cover like a giant UFO in the sky, leaving a trail of fog tangling like gauze through the brambles and coppices. During that morning smoke drivers on the national highway and the AP-7 put themselves in the hands of fate as they went through the fog banks, gripping the steering wheel in their fists and digging their nails into it, praying that the road was straight and a semi wouldn't plow into them from behind. It was then that the Vilobí airport closed its runways and sent the planes to Barcelona, and when a train could, as had happened a couple years back, pass right through the Sils station because the engineer didn't see it, and have to double back. The flat, fertile lands gained from the lake's draining had memory. Where there had once been water and where there were now fields of fodder, poplar plantations, and plane trees, the winter mornings rose wet with milky fog, and the dew's pledge—branches with pearl earrings on their tips, wisps of fodder with necklaces of crystal flowers, grains of sand with tiny diamond rings—swore evanescently that, by night, the lake would flow again.

Watching through the window as the curds of fog dispersed, he said again that, before spring, he too would emerge, renewed, from inside himself. That was why he'd come back to Vidreres, to remake his previous life, to get up each morning with the serenity of that small piece of the world on the other side of the window. It wasn't easy, but five mornings earlier luck had turned his way, and out of the fog came the car with its bloodied windows.

Had he foreseen the accident? He could smell the flesh from a distance, like the bitch whining beneath the table, still tangled in the net.

He'd spent four years away. He left Vidreres the way many rural students do, finishing high school and starting college wherever they can, just to get away from their family.

He chose fine arts because he drew well; he had a whole collection of spiral notebooks that he'd turned into comics. He made them with ball-point pens, and a few of his teachers told him he had talent. The arguing with his parents lasted months.

"You're leaving, but you'll be back," said his father. "You're an ingrate."

Nil left, convinced that getting his way with them meant he'd be able to take on the world.

He lasted a year and a half in art school. One day, when he had to turn in some stupid assignment he hadn't done, he lost it over breakfast with some dorm mates.

"Fuck academia," he said. "Fuck institutional, cookie-cutter art, fuck this bullshit."

He gave up fine arts and started to do his own thing. Nil Dalmau's first period was a tribute to the art department—he covered canvases with colorist splotches to disabuse himself of it, to purge the techniques he'd learned in class. When he saw that he wasn't getting anywhere by just reacting, he threw it all out and entered the world of digital photography, which allowed him to refute the tradition via distortions and technicalities. Nil Dalmau's second period lasted a year, and it was also a failure.

The first months with no classes and no obligations or schedule could have wrecked him, since he was used to the busy life of the farm, but they turned out to be an interesting adventure. He had to find his way in uncharted territory, both in his work and in the details of life. Without saying anything to his parents, he left the residence hall on Sardenya Street and rented a room in a shared apartment with three other artists in Poblenou. They also worked in the same divided-up studio space. He broke off contact with his art school classmates, but when he wanted to compensate by returning somewhat to his roots in Vidreres it was already too late. One weekend he went home intending to explain to his parents that he'd made a mistake by enrolling in fine arts and that now he would work under his own steam—he couldn't use words like "create" or "explore"—but while they were having lunch, excited and lively, he realized to what extent he'd separated himself from his family and his world from before college in that year and a half. How could he explain what he'd done, when, instead of the natural bond between parents and their only son, there was only a wall of mutual distrust? His parents had hardly ever left Vidreres, they had never seen an exhibition and had no desire to and, truth be told, not even he was that clear on what it meant to be an artist. What had he gotten himself into? He found out later, all too well. For the time being, he had continued to flee the denigrating hypocrisy inherent in the mere name *fine arts* and in the oppressive world of Vidreres, with no idea where he was headed. It took him another half a year to confess to his parents that he had dropped out of school.

They gave him a monthly allowance, and he lived much better than his roommates, who could barely pay rent and had to go out every day and sell themselves for sporadic small triumphs or in the miserable circuit of group shows in municipal or neighborhood exhibition spaces in deserted galleries, squats, and garages, or else throw their work out onto the Internet's global dumping ground. In a matter of a few months he saw quite a few artists hang up their brushes.

He never knew if, the next day at the studio, he'd have the same neighbor. But for him it was easier to keep going than to quit, and he had a perverse envy of those who threw in the towel. The life of the artists was like a house of mirrors in an amusement park, each one hiding behind their deformed image. He wasn't able to call it quits and go back to Vidreres, but he saw himself reflected in the others' failure. In his second period he exhibited digital photographs in bars and avoided the indifference and criticism by drinking and quarreling with artists even more desperate than he was. Who ever said making it was easy? The recession closed galleries, there were no scholarships or grants, it was no use trying to prostitute yourself by making portraits or painting still lifes or landscapes. There were no commissions of any kind, and his more creative and ambitious colleagues ended up teaching painting classes.

One night, at the bar where he was showing his work, an acting student invited him to see a Shakespeare play. When it was over he bought the book in the theater's shop. Stretched out in his room, he spent the night obsessing over the difference between the words and the play. The words were incorruptible. They had a dictionary. The next day, he put aside the exhibition he was preparing and devoted the next few months exclusively to reading—he had barely ever finished a book before. He went through authors in a week, he voraciously jumped from one to the next, and no matter how different they seemed, he made them all agree inside of him. He sat reading with a cup by his side, the book turning damp and hot in his hands, his heart marking the beat of the letters; it pumped, the sentences swelled slightly on the page and took on a red tinge, the blood seeped through the paper, it came out of the fingers on one hand and went back into the fingers of the other, irrigating his thoughts, dissolving and mixing the author's thoughts with his own, making them flow, transporting them along the channels of the printed lines. Instead of a head he had a book, and instead of a book he had a head. Those months—the autumn of two thousand and eleven—when he saw the library that was gradually growing on his shelf, it was as if he were looking at himself, standing with his back to the wall. He spent the days locked in his room, his studio mates never seeing him, not even he knew where he was; he was a shadow of the books.

Until he found he'd had enough of that lie as well— I have to be myself, that's that—and knocked down the shelf, put the books in bags, and brought them down to the dumpster. You can surrender without realizing it and have the enemy inside. But how much harm did those books do him? What did abstractions and phantasmagorical secrets have to do with him, who was of farm stock, a clean, concrete, and sensible boy, who had always had his feet firmly planted on the ground? He was weakening in every aspect. What were those challenges, those murky regions that the books explored? What was he doing, far from the fields, filling his head with fantasies and erroneous paths? No one in his family had ever gotten a degree or owned books, and they'd never missed them either, as far as he knew. He didn't save a single one. And there began Nil Dalmau's third period, the beginning of the return, the ascension, the incarnation and body art, the exteriorization, the first period that was mature and his own, which he explained to himself with this motto: disguises disguised as disguises.

A studio mate gave him the address, and he went to get his ear gauged at a hair salon in the Raval. The piercing gun fired the starting shot of a race toward himself that irrevocably distanced him from the bookish life, but also from Vidreres. It definitively amputated him from his family, but was necessary if he wanted to create something that wasn't just a series of consecutive self-deceptions. The opening in his lobe wasn't the ornamental hole in a little girl's ear, he was a prospector mining the first breach in the wall of his body, a bottomless well, a hole through which to evacuate the failure of the last few years and redeem the cowardly attempt to take refuge in books. A hole to let the world pass through, the porthole for a voyage, the flesh frame for an incorruptible, concrete work of art.

He grew his hair out and tried tattoos—he had one done on the back of his hand, where he couldn't hide it—but the tattoos had little in common with the radicalness of the Frankensteins who, every Wednesday evening, gathered at the same hair salon. He couldn't compare those people with anyone he'd ever met; strange people, people who were themselves—lives with mind-blowing value systems—fugitives of all places and all times, junkies, the mentally ill, elements of strange galaxies light years from his own. But what is art, if not that? Separating oneself, setting oneself apart, defining oneself. He started by putting in a steel earring and a discreet piercing in his other ear, joining the group of those who were masters of themselves, who singled themselves out with spiral rings in their lips, colorful piercings in their noses or eyebrows, or kilos of scrap iron hanging from their eyebrows, gums, and tongue—some had had their tongues operated on, to make them forked—their uvula, nipples, belly buttons, and all the various parts of their genitals.

The first flesh tunnel that he did was a ring, four millimeters in diameter. Flesh tunnels were a legacy of the Harappan culture, from some two thousand five hundred years before the birth of Christ. It took a week to dilate the hole in his right ear. He added earrings, at night he slept with four rings in his ear, and the weight made the hole bigger, until the morning when, in front of the mirror with his ear inflamed, red and slippery with lubricant, he was able to insert the first tunnel. The others were easier. The lobe gradually gave like a tire. The flesh tunnel he wore now was two centimeters in diameter.

His mother had bought him a car so he could come every other Sunday to Vidreres to have lunch with the family, and during those months, every time he showed up, the hole in his ear was dilated a few more millimeters. His parents couldn't imagine that he'd excavated that repulsive tunnel precisely in order to come back home with them. Through it he was regaining his confidence. His attempt to survive under his own steam had failed—it was impossible, no one managed it—he was twenty-three years old, and he had no intention of living off his parents in the city among deadbeat artists who only got younger and younger; there was no point in spending his days endlessly shooting and retouching photographs that no one was interested in. Since he couldn't emancipate himself from his family home, he'd decided to emancipate himself inside, as he finally understood his parents, grandparents, and all his ancestors had done. He wasn't living anything new. Everybody was born with blood in their veins. You can't escape your genes, you can't leave your body, but you can subjugate it, and that was how he became a comic book monster like the ones he drew in high school.

Nil Dalmau's fourth and final period, the darkest one, the incendiary one, was comprised of a series of videos that he filmed without any intention of ever exhibiting. They were a farewell to art, he wanted to bury his fears in them, bury the shame of the last few years, bury youth itself. Returning to Vidreres was the end of this project—returning to his parents' house and beginning to work the land. He would reappear like the lake reappeared in winter, gradually, naturally; recovering milieus, recovering family, recovering friends, recovering his own self. And since he couldn't imagine himself just going straight back into his parents' house, one Sunday in November he asked them for the workmen's shack in the fields of Serradell.

"I don't find any of this amusing anymore," said his father. "As far as I'm concerned, you can do what you want. If you want to move in there, you can have it by New Year's."

His father's willingness had a lot to do with the ear. Without the flesh tunnel, his father wouldn't have come up with the money or wouldn't have wanted to waste it on useless renovations. But to humiliate his son? To punish him? Here you go, failed monster, enjoy.

His mother didn't understand, or pretended not to.

"Serradell is too isolated," she said. "The only people who

ever go to the fields over there are driving the machines, for sowing or harvesting."

She thought it was dangerous because that year there'd been violent robberies in remote homes throughout the Baix Empordà, Girona, and La Selva. The thieves were breaking into farmhouses and housing developments while people were home, which was new. They would tie up the owners' wrists with telephone cords, beat them till they gave up their money and jewels, and wouldn't stop until they knew where their safe was hidden. Just a few days prior, some burglars had entered the house of a hotel owner in Platja d'Aro. They waited for it to get dark, jumped over a wall, and went through the yard and into the house where they tied up the couple. Since the man was screaming, they stuck a rag in his mouth. The man ended up suffocating. Shortly after that, in a house in Campllong, the intruders splashed two women with diesel oil from the boiler and threatened them with a lit piece of paper. In Santa Cristina, the same robbers, or some others, tied up a retired Brit, put a gun to her head, and played two rounds of Russian roulette. There was joy in these crimes; they had an artistic touch to them. They wore masks over their heads and gloves; the security cameras were useless. They carried knives, shotguns, and pistols, and they were so bold and confident that, in one attack in Llagostera, they made an omelet in the kitchen while the owner of the house was tied up in the dining room. Everyone installed alarms and filled their yards with dogs just like at Can Bou. The police hadn't caught anyone, and the burglaries continued. A crime expert published an article in the *El Punt Avui* newspaper warning of a government plot to discredit the

Catalan police force now that the regional government was becoming pro-independence.

"Nothing surprises me anymore," said his father. "Don't you watch TV, Nil? Here, everyone who can rob, does, from the king to the last patsy. Nothing can be done about it; this is a country of thieves. Look at the mess we're in. You're smart to come home. Everything is so rotten that the day things hit the fan, it will all happen at once. They're making our lives miserable, they're squeezing us on every side, and now we can't even sleep peacefully in our own homes. You're lucky. When you don't have anything, you don't have anything to worry about."

"Do you mean that, Lluís?" asked his mother. "Imagine they break into the shack and take him and call us saying that they have him and they're heading over here. What good would all the alarms in the house do us then?"

"Don't make me laugh," said his father. "If anyone breaks into the shack, it'll be the burglar who gets a nasty surprise."

His father personally supervised the bricklayers, electricians, plasterers, and painters who fixed up the shack so Nil could work and live there, with a kitchen/dining room, bathroom, fireplace, bedroom, separate workspace, and a small garage. He had the road fixed so he could drive on it with no problems. By Christmas, the renovations were completed.

Nil had been living in the shack for two weeks when the Batlle brothers were killed in that car crash.

The burial was on Monday. Tuesday afternoon, his father showed up at the shack. It was the first time he had come to see Nil. He found his son with the fireplace lit, stretched out on the sofa watching a DVD.

"I've made a very generous offer for the Batlle land," said his father. "But that doesn't mean a thing. Can Batlle is right next to Can Bou, and Iona Sureda was practically part of their family. If the Suredas play dirty, no matter how much money we offer, it won't be enough. We have to act fast. There isn't a moment to lose. I know them, at Can Bou. They have no ethics, they're poor as church mice, and they'll want to take advantage of that family's tragedy. That's not right and they know it, but we won't just stand around with our arms folded. That's why I've come to see you. Your mother would be surprised if I went out so late, and I don't want to upset her, there's no need, so it's best if she doesn't know. You'll do fine. Throw a chunk of meat filled with fishhooks or pieces of glass near the entrance to Can Bou. When they see a dog dead like that, they'll understand that this is no free-for-all."

His father's frankness caught Nil off guard, but he quickly understood what he was saying. Not upsetting his mother was an excuse. He would have liked to go further, and for a moment—a moment that he would never forget, because it could have changed everything—Nil was about to confess to his father how united they were in this venture, united by a momentous stroke of fate, by the same momentous fate by which you're born to a certain father in a certain place; he was about to tell him: You see how I never left, you see how you can be proud of me the way I am of you? But he let the moment pass, there was no need—it was out of immature selfishness, him wanting to be himself again—so he kept silent, thinking that a secret was a secret and that it had more strength incubating inside like a seed, and it would be better if his father was the one to make the overture for him to return home. He had come to him for a blood ritual, for a secret between father and son like those in every family. The Batlle lands would become the Dalmaus' through him. A generational concern. From the Batlle boys to the Dalmau boy. Years from now, he would inherit the fields, but first he would have to earn them. This was the moment. What more could he ask for? He felt very proud of his father and absolved for his attempt to flee; it was as if he were physically embracing his father, as if he carried him inside, as close to him as when he was little and rode on the tractor and his father held his shoulder as they went over the furrows.

When he was alone again, sitting on the sofa beside the fireplace, watching the silent flame gnaw on the trunks, Nil opened a beer and thought how everything was coming together: the years away from Vidreres; his return; the death of the Batlle brothers; the assignment his father had given him; and the series of videos he was filming, his farewell to artistic life. It was all compatible. Nothing was wasted. It all added up. The assignment would be a bridge between the life he was leaving behind and the one he was beginning, tying together what he'd been searching for in those years away from home with the life that awaited him. The assignment was the passport that allowed him to return as an adult to the country of his parents, his grandparents, the dead, all the people buried in the fields. And it would be recorded on video.

Euphoric with optimism, the next morning he went to buy a live lamb from a shepherd in Maçanet. The lamb left the trunk of his Honda covered in little black balls. After cleaning them up, he went to the dog pound in Tossa, and the supervisor—without asking many questions, with that idiotic respect people have for artists—helped him with the urine and lent him the protective pads, gloves, and net. That night he sacrificed the lamb. He filmed the lamb's death the way he would film the dog's, when the moment came. He would incorporate it into his project; he would make it art. He buried the lamb's skin and carcass. He put the meat he'd deboned and chopped up into a sack, tied the rag to the outside of the car door, and went to steal one of the dogs from Can Bou.

He did it in his own car despite the general alert over the robberies, excited by the idea of transgressing: not antagonism, like when he left home, not fleeing, but rather a triumph, because of the compatibility between his artwork and his father's assignment, so he risked being taken for one of those burglars who had the area so terrified.

When he finished breakfast, the fog had pretty much vanished. The bitch wouldn't stay quiet for a second. He should have finished her off the night before, as soon as he'd gotten to the shack, but he'd felt chilled and it was late—what difference would a couple of hours make?

He grabbed his coat and left to take his daily walk—the three kilometers to Lake Sils—with his eyes on the ground and a supermarket bag in his hand to gather up any animal he could find: a worm, a lizard, whatever. On Friday he'd found a wounded sparrow among some brush, blew the ants off its wings and legs, and took it with him; another day he returned to the shack with a bag full of snails that had escaped from a farm beside the road.

Crossing the highway was a bit of an adventure, but after that the walk continued peacefully through the fields. He went underneath the freeway overpass and, before reaching the small center of Sils, he took a path through ribbons of sedge, bindweed, and reeds, with poplars forming plantations that flooded every time it rained. The lake was residuary, dry in the summer and in the winter filled with migrating birds, insects, and—according to the informational panels— frogs, turtles, water voles, hedgehogs, and snakes. The last floury dust of fog scattered, the day was dawning, there were splotches of sun, and Nil's outline appeared on the path like an insect emerging from the chrysalis of fog.

At that time of day, the lake was not a solitary spot. They had reclaimed and adapted it for public use, and it was a perfect park to bring the kids to. There was always someone jogging, biking, or walking their dog on the path that went around the lake.

He knelt down to collect a beetle, but he didn't put it in the bag; he held it in his fingers, captivated by the iridescent greens on its shell. It felt soft, moving its long antennae that were as thin as hairs, tickling his hand with its six thorny legs. He pinched off one of its legs with his fingernails. When the spring came this would all be full of insects, but by then he'd already have taken refuge in his parents' house—which would later become his house—and he would have concluded and forgotten the fourth period and have no reason to want insects. He pulled off one of the beetle's wings, making it asymmetrical, a little bit like Nil with his lopsided ears. He would shave and cut off his ponytails. He would fix up his hair at the salon in Vidreres so everyone could see. He pulled another leg off the beetle. He would take out his flesh tunnel and have his ear reconstructed. He pulled the other wing off to reestablish the creature's symmetry. He would have the tattoo on his hand removed, stop collecting insects, wouldn't set foot in a dog pound ever again. His walks to the lake would turn into days of working in the terraced fields; his adventure would have come to an end, his wandering, he would never again be an artist. He dropped the beetle on the ground. It kept moving the couple of legs it still had, as if rowing, and since it couldn't flee he stepped on it and rubbed it out under his sole.

He felt sorry for the beetle. He liked the colors, shapes, and scents of those perfunctory lives, knew them physically and even knew them somewhat morally, or thought he did: they were simple, empty carcasses, they were skeletons. He could imagine how they felt, the void enclosed by the cage, how he himself would have felt without his flesh, just bones and teeth, nails and hair—the two ponytails, a wisp of beard, the tattoo, and the ring in his earlobe. If he could have extracted the flesh from inside himself, emptied himself out through his mouth and ears, remove that confusion that made him do illogical things like killing the beetle—artistic things—exterminate the viruses that led him around by the nose, set him apart, tugged on him... If we could take out our flesh from inside, expel it...

On the path around the lake there were wooden observatories for watching birds. Inside, each had a long bench beneath a narrow, glassless window that ran from one end of the belvedere to the other. The window looked out on the lake. Sometimes, if he didn't see anyone around, he would go inside and spend a while contemplating the ducks and the birds with sinuous necks, or wait for the train to pass by, the reflection of its cars on the water by the other shore. If someone came in while he was there, once the newcomer's gaze grew accustomed to the dark and found him there alone, without binoculars or a camera, with only a supermarket bag on his lap—a bag that occasionally crackled, or suddenly inflated slightly because an insect inside had jumped—with his two ponytails and his flesh tunnel, it never failed: they got up and left.

That morning he came across a high school class on a field trip, about twenty kids with two teachers Nil's age. The teachers were young, attractive women who would have been frightened by the sight of him, but he didn't mind. He'd have time to focus on girls when spring came, when his hibernation was over and he emerged from his lair. Then he'd no longer be living in the shack; he could drop by Can Bou and, without forcing anything, find himself attracted to Iona. He could count on that, and would try to make up for stealing her dog, maybe even for Jaume Batlle's death and everything else, and Nil's satisfaction would be the same as his parents'. And one day, decades later, he would confess to Iona the long road he'd taken as a young man to reach the land, which would then be three lands: Dalmau, Batlle, and Sureda.

The high school kids were thirteen or fourteen years old, surely he would be the father of kids like these by then—Nil Dalmau, in his mature fifth period—and his eldest son and heir would go out with him to their land the way he would very soon begin to go out with his father. The school group stopped and made a circle around one of the teachers, and gradually they grew quiet.

Since he was still far away, Nil left the path and approached them, discreetly, stepping softly amid the trees and brambles so they wouldn't hear him. The teacher had opened a book and spoke loudly, so the teenagers could follow her:

"You've heard the legend of the cauldrons of Pere Botero, right? Well, that happened in this area. Many, many years ago... in 1608, to be exact. That year, a farmer from Tordera named Pere Porter... Pere Porter... You see the resemblance to Pere Botero? And do you know why it mentions cauldrons? Well, because he saw them. Yes, don't laugh. He saw them because he went down into hell... and he entered hell right around here. Do you see this book? It's an edition of the anonymous manuscripts that tell the story of Pere Porter. Pere Porter was a farmer who was forced to repay a debt that he'd already paid, because of an evil notary... it was some sort of a scam, you get it? And Pere went to Maçanet to look for the money demanded from him and came across a young man on horseback, pulling another horse behind him, and they went on the road together. As they walked, Pere Porter explained what was going on with him, and when they reached Lake Sils, Pere asked if he could ride the other horse. And the young man said he could and... Now be very quiet, and I'll read you what happened. Pay attention, because it's old Catalan. 'Porter crossed himself, and when he mounted the horse it all changed: every hair on his head rose as he heard and saw the steeds speaking with one another...' His hair stood on end because the horses started talking to each other! And then the young man said he would take Pere to see the evil notary who hadn't recorded the payment of his debt...and you know where he was, right? Where do you think that evil notary was?"

"In hell?" said a girl.

"That's right, he was in hell. 'Hence,' the young man said, 'hold tight to that steed, for I am the devil!'"

The teacher had adopted a deep voice to imitate the devil, and the students laughed. She continued reading, slowly, so no one would miss a thing:

"'Porter, hearing those words, said: "Jesus, save me, don't forsake me, Blessed Virgin, be with me." And thereupon...,' which means at that point, the horses: 'both steeds proceeded through the lake, mountains, valleys, talking all the while...' The horses talked, they talked the whole time they took Pere to hell, what do you think? Can you imagine what they were saying to each other?"

What would animals say as they carried you off to hell? What was the beetle saying as I dismembered and squashed it, what had the bitch been saying all night long; what was it saying right now, locked up in the shack, tangled in the net? He saw a worm on a leaf. It must talk like a little snake. He collected the worm and put it in the bag. He turned over another leaf and peeled a snail off it. He kicked over a rock. Underneath, it was filled with earwigs and damp beetles, which he gathered and put into the bag.

"And do you know what Pere Porter was doing?" continued the teacher. "Well, he was holding on 'tight to the mount. After an hour on horseback, having passed great valleys, great mountains, great rivers, and great seas, they entered the mouth of a cave and then egressed'—which means that they went out—'onto a great plain that was all fire and demons, with multitudes of people.'"

That was when a boy in the group turned excitedly toward him, and Nil felt exposed. He crouched down, then fled with his head bowed like a chastened animal. He walked through the trunks, got tangled in the brambles, and when he raised his head again he realized that the boy hadn't been startled by him, but by what Nil now saw before him: a hot-air balloon, inflated but still on the ground, that peeked out above some trees on the other side of the road.

The plain functioned as a base camp for the balloons; it was an ideal place for them to take off and land. A great plain that was all fire and demons, once flooded and centuries later drained for plant terraces and woodlands. The top of the balloon emerged above and a bit to one side of the tree branches; in fact, it looked like another tree, a colorful tree in the bloom of spring, and Nil crossed the road—he heard a couple of horns honking behind him but didn't turn—and kept making his way to the shack before changing direction to get a better look at the balloon. He came out from the trees and approached it; they had inflated it in the middle of a barren field; there were two cars, a van, and a man who was watching the seven passengers in the basket about to take off. The pilot lifted his arms every once in a while with two lit flares, two vertical columns of fire, which he stuck into the belly of the balloon to heat up the air. The passengers—four adults, two kids, and the pilot—waved good-bye to the man who had remained on the ground, and when the pilot lit the fire, the jets of helium roared, and two luminous horns showed through the balloon's fabric.

A great plain that was all fire and demons, and the balloon detached from the field and began to move horizontally, at first slowly and floating only just above the ground, walking, running as if carried by a breeze that didn't move a single branch, that Nil couldn't feel on his skin, and then it passed alongside a group of poplars and climbed diagonally toward the sky.

Planes out of the Vilobí airport were flying higher up; Nil followed them with his gaze as he waited to hear the bursts of fire from the balloon. The fire was light, painters were pyromaniacs, all artists were, he himself was a demon, working in fire... But who knew, deep down, what he was. An artist? A demon? What is a demon? What does *demon* mean? Who knows if a murderer can ever become a murderer within himself, even if he wants to; who knows what we might find all the way inside a word. Words are traitors, they're full of dregs; action, on the other hand, is luminous, it can be filmed.

He heard the bitch's moaning before he reached the door of the shack. He opened it and saw the animal, still caught in the net. She had dragged herself from under the table to beside the fireplace. When the bitch saw him she reacted. She couldn't move, but she lowered her eyes—she knew who was in charge—and was quiet for a moment, but then that unbearable whimpering began again.

Nil had no time to waste. He had gotten too distracted by the balloon; he had to empty the bag. He put the plug into the kitchen sink, poured the insects in, and watched the costume ball of beetles, grasshoppers, the earwigs he had found under the rock, the centipedes he'd grabbed crossing the road, spiders, snails, praying mantises, and ants, all hugging the steel dance floor… Along the way there had been fights and deaths in the bag, and the hurly-burly in the sink was disturbing. He wanted to turn on the tap to give those empty little boxes stuffing, flesh, but it was just that emptiness that meant it would be hard to drown them—they would float like a raft of tiny pieces, a mosaic of colors.

He started by separating out the grasshoppers, who were big and had quickly freed themselves from the other critters and were jumping about the kitchen. He scooped them up and used a funnel to get them into a plastic bottle. He had half a bottle full. Then came the beetles, and then the backswimmers, the worms, and the snails, each type in their own container. Once the separating was done, he covered the bottles with perforated tops, put them in a cardboard box, and took them to his workspace on the other side of the wall.

He went back into the dining room. The bitch tried to roll over, like a fish. Her claws had gotten stuck in the strings, and she'd made a mess of the net with her legs. Nil put on gloves and covered one arm with protective padding, and he cut a hole in the net with a bread knife so the animal could get its head through. The dog growled and sunk her teeth into the arm pad. He let her. After she tired herself out, he put a muzzle on her. Then she didn't moan because she couldn't, but she started to whine. Maybe it was her leg, or maybe she had a broken bone; he tightened the muzzle with five layers of packing tape.

II

At midday he was in the parking lot of El Capitell restaurant, on the outskirts of Bescanó. The place had been closed for months, but you could see the building better from the highway now than when the restaurant was in business, because over each of the three windows on the ground floor, which was the dining area, they'd hung large independentist flags as curtains. The independentist movement had upended the power balance—Nil's parents had hung the starred flag at their house, and he would have put one up at the shack, except no one ever passed by in Serradell.

On the door of the closed restaurant hung a sign that said FOR RENT / FOR SALE, with a cell phone number. As he maneuvered into the empty parking lot, Nil saw a flag-curtain lift slightly, and an old man peeked out from behind the glass. Nil got out of the Honda and walked to the door. He found it locked, but since he'd seen the man, he knocked on the glass. Nothing moved inside. He knocked a few more times, then sat down on the entrance steps. The highway was very empty and the few cars raced by. He got tired of waiting. He went back to the door and knocked harder and harder. He could see the keys hanging from the inside lock; he tried to force the door and knocked some more. The blows reverberated in the empty dining room. If he kept knocking like that, he would break the glass.

"What do you want?" the old man finally shouted from behind the door.

"I'm Nil Dalmau, I've come for the tables! We have an appointment!"

The old man approached the glass, shaking his head.

"You must have talked to my son-in-law!"

Nil was used to these roles. "The truck's coming now!" he said.

It seemed that the old man was calming down, but he shook his head again. "Where's the truck?" he shouted.

"I said it's on its way! Can you show me the tables?"

"Haven't you seen the photos?"

"Hey!" shouted Nil. "Do you want to sell the tables or not?"

The old man hesitated for a moment, and then shook his head yet again.

"Are you saying you had me come all the way here for nothing?" asked Nil.

Just then the truck arrived. Miqui stopped in the middle of the parking lot and, without turning off the engine, hopped down from the cab and came over to shake Nil's hand.

"Should I bring the truck closer?" he said.

"Wait, there's a problem," said Nil, pointing with his chin to the old man behind the door. "He doesn't want to open up."

"He doesn't want to open up?" Miqui went over to the door to talk to the old man. "Good morning! What's wrong?"

"Nothing. We just changed our minds."

"What's that?"

Nil also approached the door. He had ten fifty-euro bills fanned out in his hand.

"Do you think we'd bring you the money if we were planning anything bad?" he said.

The old man hesitated again. His hand was already on the knob, but he stopped, lowered his head, approached the glass, and said:

"I can't. We've got coffeemakers in here, refrigerators, machinery... I can't risk it, it's all we have. The faucet factory closed down, we used to get the workers in for lunch every day. But there's no cash register, no safe. My son-in-law left me here alone. I can't open up. He would never forgive me. Come back later today, he'll be here, he's usually here, but this morning they called and he had to go to the bank... The bank calls the shots, it's not his fault. Come back this afternoon, please, let's do it that way. I'm sure he'll give you a discount."

"Open up," demanded Miqui. "We're good people, for fuck's sake!"

They could have broken the glass door with one kick. The old man was starting to sweat. He pulled a cell phone out of his pocket.

"Come back this afternoon, please," he said. "Leave, or I'll call the police."

"You know what?" burst out Miqui. "You're fucking with us. Don't call the police, because if you call the police, I'm going to come back some day and do something that'll make you and your son-in-law never want to fuck with anybody again. Who do you think you are? Screw you and your fear! I've had it with old people who think they're the kings of the world! I have a job, I make an honest living, you hear me? Do you know what it costs, just in gas, to get here in my truck? You think I'm loaded or something? You think I have nothing better to do with my time? Have a little respect, goddamn it. No one fucks with me, you got that? Open the fucking door right now, or I'll break the glass and come in myself to get the tables. Put down that phone!"

The old man started to dial, and Nil grabbed Miqui by the arm. He didn't know whether his threats were serious or not. He pulled him away from the door, signaling to the old man to calm down.

"Don't call, please," said Nil, and he came back over to the door, making sure to turn his face to show his good ear. "We'll come back later when your son-in-law is here. I'm interested in the tables. We'll come back this afternoon when your son-in-law is here, no problem."

The old man looked up from the cell phone and said, yes, they needed the money, but as he wiped his forehead with a handkerchief his eyes widened like saucers and the cell phone dropped to the floor. The trucker was pointing a shotgun at them from the door of his truck.

As Miqui approached the door with the barrel raised, it became clear that he was threatening the old man. But Nil didn't take that for granted at first. Nearly anyone who had to choose between shooting a frightened old man and a freak like him wouldn't hesitate. His tunnel was provocative, being different was provocative, and even more so outside of Barcelona. Leaving the herd made you stronger, but it provoked other people: strength is as effective a provocation as weakness. Now that the starred independentist flags were the majority, their presence incited the other flags. But it was misleading—difference, when exposed, lost strength. Any form of expression weakened it. Maybe he would pay the price for wanting to speak with his body—without words or gestures, with physical, permanent, and solitary actions—for having been foolish enough to turn inward. What was he looking for by playing the artist, to turn inward until there was nothing left? And the end would be his disappearance? Ending up flat out with a bullet in his chest at the door of a closed restaurant in Bescanó? And the earring, the fires, what were they? Signs leading to him?

In less than a second he could be lying beside the two boys killed in the accident. In less than a second he could have more in common with the Batlle brothers than with any sucker who was still breathing. The old man in that restaurant, the grasshoppers and worms he collected, the guy with the shotgun, the bitch locked in the shack, the family in the balloon, Iona Sureda, his father, the fucking poplar plantations would have more in common with each other than with him. The land they'd left behind had more life in it than the two boys. Even as he was crushing it, the wingless, legless beetle's life was worth infinitely more than all the human and nonhuman lives that had been snuffed out since the universe began. Supposedly, he was involved in a gambit to become an heir, to embody a succession—he'd had a stroke of luck. But now that land might be used to bury him. Damn immortal land. What would happen to the fields? Who would inherit them? That desertion, that lack of an owner—that was death.

He wanted some steel tables, and he had needed someone to transport them. On Tuesday, he was at the club with Iona, and this Miqui showed up like a godsend, giving him a business card. Like a godsend. Now he might blow him away by squeezing his finger half a centimeter. His mother had been right. The shack was a bad idea. Without the shack he wouldn't have come back to Vidreres, without the shack he wouldn't have thought about setting up a workspace, he wouldn't have needed the tables, and a nut wouldn't be aiming a shotgun at him. In the four years away from home, the year and a half surrounded by weirdos, he'd never seen anything like this. Ah, but then he had been among his people! And now, where was he? In no-man's-land, neither here nor there. There was nothing he could do: death always comes without warning, that's the only way it can catch you, always by accident; even for the terminally ill death has to be a surprise, it catches you by surprise or it doesn't get you. Tell that to the animals he collected in the mornings or that he picked up at the pound, tell that to the bitch he had in his shack, or to the Batlle brothers. He was about to enter that world shared by people, animals, and plants, where life was the same for everyone: zero. Where did this Miqui person come from? Why was he carrying a shotgun? Had he been looking for Nil? Was he part of one of the groups of thieves who had the remote homes so frightened, who made their owners check the windows, doors, and blinds, who made the whole family hush if the littlest brother thought he heard some slight sound, maybe some footsteps, something falling to the floor—I heard it perfectly, said the boy, and I'm scared—so the family kept still, waiting in silence, with their eyes wide and their fingers crossed, to see if someone really had broken into the house . . . With that same attention, with that microscopic precision, with his ears pricked up, with the vibration of his metal tunnel in the surrounding flesh he would hear the click of the trigger that would release the hammer and expel the bullet. That's how death approaches, by surprise, always uncertainly, never sure.

Once he was dead, his parents would lock up the shack. They would let the bitch go. She would run, limping and moaning in pain, back to Can Bou. What good is the land, his father would say, when, without children, it's worthless? I'm tired of it all! This time for real! Now I know true disgrace! And why? What is this, a punishment? Haven't I had enough, seeing it happen to my neighbor twice over? Do I have to go through it myself? Me? A truck shows up at the shack, his parents wait by the door, it's there to take away the furniture, the extractor hoods, the clothes, the shoes, the camera, the computer with his videos . . . What are these bottles, Lluís? Some of them are still alive! Is this what my son spent his time doing? Collecting insects? Where did he learn to do that? And why? Why did he do it, Lluís? And why did he come back so strange and unsociable? What happened to him in Barcelona? Why did he do that to his ear? And the videos? Why can't I see them? Was our son crazy? Is that why he came back to Vidreres—to get killed?

But the shotgun ignored Nil. The old man opened the door, crying, and the two guys went in. Nil picked up the cell phone off the floor, locked the door behind him, put the key in his pocket with the phone, and asked the old man if the tables were in the kitchen.

They went through the empty dining room and there were the tables, of course, the same wide, heavy tables he had seen in the photograph online before calling the man's son-in-law. Miqui and Nil carried them to the entrance, and from the entrance to the truck. They put them on the flatbed with the crane and tied them down for the trip.

Nil went back into the restaurant for a moment. The old man was sitting at a table with his head in his hands. Nil placed the money beside him, with the cell phone and keys on top. The man didn't dare lift his head.

Miqui was waiting for Nil, smoking, beside the truck. He'd leaned the gun against one wheel. Anyone passing on the highway, a police squad car, could have seen the shotgun.

"Artists," muttered Nil.

The truck followed him to Serradell. They unloaded the tables with the crane just as they had loaded them up and brought them into the workspace. They put them in the empty spot beneath the extractor hood.

"Are you a chef?" asked Miqui. Then he saw the tripod and camera. "You take photos? Photos of food?"

"Videos. Shorts. I'm an artist."

"I admire artists."

"They're more common than you think. Do you want to see the tables get their first run? I owe you a favor."

He brought Miqui a chair and asked if he wanted a beer. He focused the camera on the table. He turned on the lights, lowered the blinds, and hauled a cardboard box filled with plastic bottles out of the closet. He pulled out two and emptied them onto the middle of the largest table. He tapped the bottom of the bottles so the little black rocks inside would come out. They were beetles of varying sizes, which came to life on the table. Some of them seemed dead but weren't, they were playing dead, trying to protect themselves that way. Others curled up right where they'd fallen, and still others ran over the edge of the table and fell to the floor.

He spritzed the largest group with a spray bottle and then splashed a rain of alcohol all over the table. The smell spread through the workshop. He turned on the extractor, started recording, and turned off the lights. He pulled a lighter out of his pocket, lit it, and brought it over to the largest beetle. The beetle burst into flame. The fire leaped from one shell to the next. The beetles ran with their fire, crashing into each other, spreading the small blue flame, turning into little rocks of light, then quickly going out.

He ran a brush along the steel, making the black dust fall to the floor, then emptied a couple more bottles out onto the table. The spiders burned faster than the beetles; they made one big flash and disappeared, consumed amid the smoke. They held up a flaming topaz on eight skinny legs. It lasted an instant. Just enough time for it to fix on your retina if you quickly closed your eyes. The image remained there for a few seconds, a luminous sketch of spider tattooed on the inside of your eyelid, until it too vanished.

He dumped out a mix of insects from another bottle, backswimmers, earwigs, ladybugs, praying mantises, and grasshoppers that leaped like sparks when they were set afire. They had parabolas of light over the embers of little legs and segments, jaws, hair, spikes, horns, wings, and antennae. He swept the table again and emptied more bottles. The worms twisted with their tips in the air, little red-hot horseshoes, lengths of live coal and then ash. Nil filmed the cloud of blue sparks from fleas; he lit up the evanescent galaxy of an anthill, ephemeral constellations of mosquitoes, hawker dragonflies on fire, damselflies and horseflies, bees that fell like a meteor shower, blue blowflies... He pulled out a box from a pet shop. The lid was green mesh. He spritzed what was inside right through the mesh. He uncovered the box and out flew tropical butterflies with large wings, which he lit up with the lighter like the pages of a book. The colorful glitter made a short flight before scorching and melting into the darkness.

When Nil turned on the light, Miqui applauded.

"Amazing," he said, "I swear, never seen anything like it. They must pay you well."

Nil shook his head as he stopped the camera and started to sweep up.

"It's a labor of love?" Miqui thought it over for a moment then said, "What a weird hobby. Post it online and you'll get a million hits."

"There are animal protection laws."

"For spiders and flies? For butterflies? Are you saying you've done this with bigger animals?"

Nil turned the lights off again. He had his laptop connected to a wide-screen television. He switched it on. It was a film that was shot at night in the field in front of the shack. The camera gradually adapted to the darkness and focused on a shadow that became a lamb, a lamb tied by its neck to the ground, probably to a rock in the middle of the field. The camera remained in one spot. The elf with the hole in his ear came out with a container on his back connected by a tube to a spray gun. He approached the lamb and soaked it. Then he rubbed the liquid in with his fingers. Before untying the lamb, he kneeled down for a moment on the other side of the animal, where he lit something—a wick—then ran out of the frame.

"Here's where the film will start once it's edited," Nil said.

Light appeared behind the lamb. The animal turned its head, looked at its thigh, and started to run in circles. The fire spread through its wool. In a matter of seconds the entire lamb was aflame and galloping through the field, streaking it with light. It fell, extended its legs with a tremble, then stopped, immobile. It kept burning until it went out on its own, amid a cloud of smoke.

He had dozens of videos, an encyclopedia; the lamb was the last one he had shot, but there were videos of cats on fire who bristled suddenly like a balls of flame, jumping with panicked yowls; he had dogs, running with just their tails on fire at first, then all of them, packs of dogs fleeing through the woods, always at night, hunting dogs, as if desperately chasing some prey, but all they were chasing was an escape from themselves, from their pain; and birds, thrown off a cliff, that flapped their wings of light four or five times—not to fly but to put out the flames, though only stoking them—until they collapsed suddenly like meteorites toward the depths of the abyss. And a snake that shot across the ground like a gilded arrow; a rabbit that hopped through the dry brush, leaving paths of flame in its wake. He had projects thought up that he wouldn't get a chance to do, fields of flowers with their corollas on fire, fruit burning up on the branches, palm trees, forests, galloping horses of fire, herds of flaming goats climbing cliffs, bulls, peacocks, roosters, cows burning in green fields, fiery ducks and swans swimming, men and women and children dressed in flames.

"You could make money off all this," said Miqui. "We could commercialize it; there's no risk, I can tell you that. If you don't need the money, think about other people for a second."

Nil didn't answer, and in that silence the bitch's wail could be heard through the door.

"More material," said Miqui.

"That's my dog. It's dinnertime, he's hungry."

"Why don't we talk about it, the Internet thing? Why don't you let me look into it, and we can give it a try? We can do it from a server in India or the ends of the earth. I don't think it's illegal, at least not with the fleas and a few fucking beetles, that'd be ridiculous, but it's got a morbid appeal, I'm sure it would work, people love sick shit."

"No. I don't want any problems."

"What if I buy it off you?"

"You don't need to buy it. You can do it yourself. I'll let you have the idea."

"I'm no artist, Nil," said Miqui. "I never would have thought that up. Let me look into it this afternoon. Don't pay me for the trip, man. Let's get together later. I'll come pick you up. I have some girlfriends, I'll introduce you to them, you should unwind a little, you seem worked up, we'll relax and talk business and you'll see things differently. I'll come get you at eleven, OK?"

The bitch on the other side of the door was getting louder and louder. Nil nodded; he'd have a lot to celebrate tonight.

The bitch had been rubbing her snout against the net and had managed to detach some of the packing tape. Even so, Nil stretched out on the sofa and dozed off after lunch. He slept for a couple of hours straight—his dreams squashed deep down inside him—until the bitch woke him up again. When it got dark he would put her down. That was the end of it. He would give the short films to the trucker, and he could do whatever he wanted with them. He would give him the camera and the laptop with the photographs from his second period, and then they would go celebrate with the girls.

The bitch was still and looking intently at the door, exhaling hard through her snout with her ears tensed but not lifted, because of the constraints of the net. Nil went over to look out the window. It was the end of the afternoon, and there was thin fog that would vanish at dusk; it was a prelude that gave way to the thicker fog. He'd learned to watch it as he waited for night to fall, a fake fog that could just as easily have come from the fires of farmers as from steam escaping from the ATO milk processing plant, or from the tanker trucks that constantly came to Vidreres to fill their steel tanks at the plant in the industrial park.

Shit. Someone was coming along the path, and it could only be his father. The shack wasn't anywhere that people just passed by, it was at the end of the path. He couldn't pretend he wasn't there, because his car was parked outside. His father wouldn't be pleased to find out that he'd taken the dog with him instead of killing it at Can Bou. Nil wouldn't have an easy time explaining it either. He quickly grabbed the packing tape to wrap up the bitch's muzzle again. He still had time to drag her into the workshop. But he took another look out the window. The person approaching was Iona, from Can Bou.

Shit. But better Iona than his father. He grabbed his coat, left the shack, and walked quickly over to her. He stopped her far enough away that she wouldn't hear the bitch.

"I'm looking for a dog," said Iona, "her name is Seda, she's been missing all day. I thought maybe you'd seen her, maybe she headed this way, she must be really lost. She's got a bad limp, we found her injured on the road..."

"If you got her off the road, she must have gone back to her owners. Dogs do that, it seems like they've gotten used to you, but one day they wake up and go back home."

Iona's hair was shiny, her skin taut and porous; she had bags under her eyes from crying, but the pupils darted around. Nil thought about the pretty young teachers he'd seen that morning and the trucker's friends awaiting him that night. Would he eventually get used to this girl? Would he really like her? When spring came, Iona would have to forget about the bitch and about Jaume. He himself will have changed a lot by then, he won't be like he is now.

"How's it going, life in the shack?" she said.

"Come some other day and I'll show you," Nil said. "I was just leaving."

But Iona didn't move. She had to make an effort to say what came next:

"One question, Nil. Why did you show me that video?"

"I made a mistake. You're right, I shouldn't have. It wasn't the right moment. I just wanted to be there for you."

"Be there for me?"

"I wanted to be there for you in your grief. I'm trying to adapt to being here again, fit in. I don't know anything about anyone. I've been gone a long time."

Iona took in a deep breath—Nil perfectly heard her take it in—and suddenly took off running toward the shack.

"I just have to see for myself!" she screamed in a cracked voice as she ran. "I can't leave without checking! I have to check, Nil! I have to see it for myself!"

Shortly afterward, as she walked past him with the bitch in her arms, still tangled in the net—"sick fuck!" and the bitch showing him her teeth, Iona having removed the packing tape, "fucking asshole!"—Nil thought that he could have locked the door but he hadn't.

He brooded over whether to take his car and go to the butcher shop, or buy nails and smash up a piece of glass, or get some rat poison, or just ask the trucker to do it with his shotgun, on their way back from seeing the girls, in exchange for the videos.

He didn't have long to think it over. Iona had only just disappeared down the path when he saw another figure approaching, a figure very similar to himself, except for the ear—the last person he wanted to see right then. The gait was identical to his own. Nil walking toward Nil.

His father had his hands in his pockets and planted himself in front of Nil without any greeting.

"I didn't call so your mother wouldn't ask questions. I've

been expecting *you* to call *me* with some excuse. But you haven't said a word all day. And now I see the girl from Can Bou leaving here, crying, carrying a dog trapped in a net. You'd better have a good explanation. Because if this is what I think it is, you really screwed up, Nil. I hope you have an explanation. You had that dog, didn't you? You didn't carry it off in a net! And the dog was injured. Do you mind telling me what that girl was doing here, crying and picking up an injured dog at our shack? Can you explain it, or is there no need? You know what's going to happen, right? They're going to report us. I'll say this in case you don't already understand: it's over. There's no way we can get the land now. Did you hear me, Nil?"

His father grabbed him by the shoulders. He shook him and asked him to explain himself. Nil couldn't say anything; his father was right. They'd spent four years waiting for him. In four years, they'd only had one bit of good news: when they found out he'd quit art school. When he told them they didn't hide their happiness—an underwater power cable that connected him and his parents, but didn't start to work until his father asked him to go kill a dog at Can Bou. For four years, his parents worried that their son would never come back from Barcelona. Every month they paid him the salary that it would take three black men working sun up to sun down to earn, as his father told him one day; they paid so he could devote himself to searching for another world, to betraying them, with the hope that he would grow tired of it. His parents had also acted irresponsibly. They had to have some fault in it, letting him go, letting him get mixed up in a lie. Or was it an experiment? Had they sent him out to explore? Go, see if you find anything better. Go, fail, grow up, you'll be back. And when his father pushed him, Nil pushed back, and they started to fight. A father and son don't reach this point so easily. His father was carrying a lot of rage inside, and every blow that Nil took was worth ten, the punches came as if pressurized—his father was strong, a man of the earth, a rock from the field, the wait had turned long and tense, waiting every day while he watched other people's children living according to God's plan, taking up the reins, continuing, who was Nil to leave and then fail—and every time Nil received a blow from his father there was a reason behind it, and he just let himself be shook and beat on, he didn't struggle against it, he'd thought of his father every morning when he saw the Batlle brothers heading out into the fields with theirs ... And when his father grew tired and stopped, Nil got up in pain and helped his father to stand.

"You're all the same, Nil," his father said, "everybody your age is the same. You scammed us. You played us for fools. You took advantage of us. You know what hurts us the most, Nil? We were afraid that one day we'd open the newspaper and see that they were talking about you, about the things you were doing. That we'd find out that you were even further into the lie, that you believed it completely. We helped you because you're our only child, and there was no other option—your teachers said you were intelligent and that your mother and I had to have a lot of patience—and we didn't lose hope even though we saw it coming for a long time. Parents always have to think the worst; we need to see it coming. Look at the Batlles. We knew you wanted to go to college, so we let you do it because it wasn't a question of four years or even eight . . . but to work here you don't need a degree, you need effort and know-how, real know-how, not that flighty left-wing crap they fill your head with, the ideas they started giving you really young . . . What kind of artist could come out of Vidreres? . . . Before books and before artists there was the land, and someone was working it, and when there are no books left, or artists, or paintings, or any of that shit, because one day all of that will be history, like everything else . . . do you know what will still be here? The land will still be here. Scratch at it all you like, throw a bomb at it and you'll make a hole, and underneath there'll be more. Your grandfather always said, when he was little, in the war, they took land to build an aviation field. You see what's left of that field. You can scratch at it all you like, you can throw a bomb, but under the dirt there's more dirt. You kids think you're so smart. You're so full of yourselves. You lasted a year, Nil, you dropped out and we thought: well, he'll be back here soon. But then it only got worse: you didn't come back right away, and then one day you show up with that ear. I'm still not used to it. That's our flesh, goddamn it! And then you asked me for the shack. Your mother didn't want to—women know more about these things—she'd given you up for lost, not like me. I'm just a poor man, and when the boys from Can Batlle got themselves killed, the only thing I could think of was to ask you to do a job that I should've done myself. I thought I could treat you like a grown-up. I don't know why you wanted the shack, I don't know and I don't care what you've been doing in there, I haven't stuck my nose into it, I haven't asked any questions. All I asked was for you to look out for the family and the land and . . . How could you have blown this bit of luck, luck that could help our family survive for a hundred more years? A hundred more years, Nil. Does that not seem like much to you? Or you think it's too much? You didn't have to do it for yourself; it was about those that'll come after you, you hear me, all the dead are in these fields . . . You really screwed up, Nil. Now the land will go to the Suredas, and Can Bou will grow. Goddamn it. At least those two killed themselves. It shouldn't have been them that died. But what do you know, you, who left the land? You live in a world that's about to explode—we've sold you kids out, let you do what you want. Now I understand why you didn't say anything, now I see why the earring, why you wanted to lock yourself away here . . . just to escape, because that's all you know how to do!"

One night, fifteen years earlier, Nil was sitting with his parents in front of the fireplace. They were watching a game show on TV. First they heard a wheeze and then a roar, as if there were a beast stuck in the chimney, roasting. There was no animal. Their chimney had caught fire. Nil's father jumped up from his chair, and his mother ran to move the sofa. His father came out of the kitchen with a bucket of water. He put out the fire in the hearth, then ran upstairs with another bucketful and Nil's mother behind him. Nil was eight years old. He couldn't think of anything better to do than to put his head into the fireplace. He crouched down, leaned against the hot, black water and, burning his cheek against the still-scorching tile, looked upward like he sometimes did when there was no fire blazing. During the day you could see the light all the way at the top, like the reflection in the bottom of a well, and you heard very precise sounds from outside the house, which traveled through the air from far away—as if the chimney were a small, long shell, an antenna to pick up the barks of dogs from other houses, the occasional shout from a neighboring field, or the engine of a motorcycle—sounds separated from their place, exiled like the dim light you could see all the way at the top; light from the sky separated from the sky. That night he hadn't expected to see the placid light of day, nor even a bit of moonlight, but he also hadn't expected the nest of snakes that he did see. A virulent flaming light, frantic between the black walls, a well in hell that made the whole house tremble. He felt a hot splatter on his arm, a bit of soot had fallen into the puddle of water on the floor. Sparks fell from all the way up the chimney, floating down like incandescent, volatile rain, and he had to move out from under them. Then he ran upstairs to his parents, wanting them to protect him; throughout the whole house the chimney's snoring could be heard, like a flute, *zuuuu*, *zuuu*, and it seemed the walls were quivering in a sustained, never-ending earthquake, and Nil went up the staircase along the chimney, running his hand along the wall's plaster. And it was hot, it was burning hot, the fire was just on the other side, a few centimeters away from him. He was afraid that the whole house would suddenly burst into flames, and he saw a crack in the plaster that hadn't been there before, long and deep and all the way up to the ceiling, and he went out on the roof, and there he found his father, who'd just thrown a bucket of water into the chimney but stood still, as if hypnotized. The chimney was a small volcano, a fountain of sparks that the wind carried into the night over the fields, into the fresh air. The fire gradually died out, fewer and fewer sparks falling onto the adobe roof, bouncing, and being carried off by the wind . . .

Now his father left without saying a word, through the fields, disheartened after the fight, cursing and defeated.

Light pricked the hills; the red sky turned violet and increasingly opaque. The clouds made maps of continents with peninsulas, islands, and coastline, a shadow of the earth's continents, black ash that would fall on the fields and make them barren, enslave them, and then the night's water would turn it all to mud.

The moon focused on Serradell; Nil was sitting at the door to the shack, lost in his labyrinths. He had a long glass tube and a jar with a mix of water and flammable paste. He was blowing bubbles and lighting them on fire. His planets of lava and blood floated over Serradell, dying out here and there.

Why did you do all that? Because you're a pyro? For your own pleasure? For the light, for the exorcism of death that the deaths of others brings—since they leave and you stay and make a record of it, you make their deaths material in your videos and make material of death? Because you want to construct a garment of death, wrap yourself in these deaths so when your moment comes you're prepared? Are you searching for the light that will consume you? Exploring art's extreme limits? Do you think there's nowhere further to go—nothing beyond here—and it only makes sense to turn back, to pack it in? Why did you do it? To satisfy your imagination? Because you were lonely? Because it was as if you were burning yourself up? Did you do it because you couldn't explain it?

Would he be brave enough to pack his bags and leave? He admired so many painters, had seen so many exhibitions in those four years, and beyond each painting and each video there were entire museums of paintings and videos that hadn't been made and were worth more because of that. Walls and blank walls. Artwork without pain. Full stillness. Blameless sin. He could have lived with that emptiness, but wasn't brave enough; he searched until he found a way, and he started to kill animals as a path to return home, to an earthly state, the same state that his father sought with his work each day by turning his body into his land, going into the field like a worm to eat his own flesh; every single day, with the obsession that his son would continue so the flesh and the land could be the same, and in this perpetuation his existence was at stake, the existence of his ancestors, life itself was at stake.

The truck's headlights approached like eyes getting a closer look at him. He heard the engine, the big wheels, sounds that had nothing to do with what the same engine and the same wheels did during the day—there were day sounds and night sounds, and the ones at night were more precise and fine-tuned—two types were needed, one to watch over the other, like the two headlights on the truck, two types in symmetry, just as with the body: hands, feet, brain hemispheres, the same symmetry as with the dead brothers.

Miqui was waiting for him in the cab. He gestured for him to climb in.

"Ready to have some fun?" he asked, when Nil was inside. "Good news—I looked into the Internet thing. There's no problem."

He had a photo of a naked girl taped next to the steering wheel, with huge, symmetrical tits.

"Our Lady of Safe Travels," said Miqui. "Wait till you see Cloe and Marga."

"You have to take me to Lake Sils," said Nil.

"You want to go to the lake now? Wait until we come back . . . if you still want to then!"

"Take me there."

"There's two of them, Nil . . . it's gonna take some time!"

They were passing the tree. In the truck's headlights, the bouquet looked like a bride's bouquet.

"What assholes," said Miqui.

"A lot of accidents are suicides and no one realizes," said Nil. "We don't know anything about other people's pain."

Miqui gave him a puzzled look. "Is something going on with you?"

Nothing is more closely guarded than the pain we cause ourselves. We don't talk about it, and we try not to think about it, but the pain accrues. The worst pain is what we do to ourselves. We know where it'll hurt. And the dead turn over in their graves and don't forgive the living for not taking advantage of what they've lost forever. They don't forgive us for living in hell; they don't forgive the zoo of animals that the living burn inside themselves, that madness.

"I don't want to go see the girls," said Nil. "Just drop me off at the lake, and I'll walk back on my own. I'll give you the videos. You can do whatever you want with them."

Miqui exited the national highway and took the Sils road.

"You didn't understand me," said Miqui. "I want you to come with me. What could you possibly have to do at the lake at this time of night? We have a date with the girls, we're late, you can't be rude with chicks. What's wrong with you?"

They turned off onto an unpaved road before reaching the center of Sils.

"You want me to leave you here?" said Miqui. "At this time of night? You are really fucking weird, Nil. You want me to go with you? You want me to wait for you?"

"Piss off," said Nil, and he got out of the cab.

But Miqui turned off the engine.

"You can leave," said Nil. "Go."

The truck lit up the road. Nil lifted his arm, nodded good-bye, and began walking. He heard the road in the distance, and the freeway, and the jet engines of a plane. He heard croaks and animal noises from the water. And then a honk made Nil turn around. Miqui had lowered the window and was aiming at him from the cab.

"Get back in the truck," said Miqui.

"Piss off," Nil said again.

And he saw the flare leave the mouth of the barrel, and there was a very brief silence, then a deafening thunderclap immediately followed by dirt and a laugh that skated over the lake's water.

"Nobody tells me to piss off!" shouted Miqui, and he turned on the engine. "Got that? Nobody! You're out of your mind, Nil! You're nutty as a fruitcake, a fucking fruitcake! Look at this shotgun! I'd never shoot anybody! I'm not like you, with your fucking freak ear! You're mental! You're out of your fucking mind!"

Nil remained motionless until the truck was far away, and then took the path he always did around the lake. The cold compressed reality: there was an effervescence of stars around the moon, the black glass of the sky was filled with little holes so you could see through to the other side; with one kick he'd shatter it to pieces. He took the same path as always, his place was here, at night—the darkness, the cold, the solitude. He heard a train coming and went into one of the observatories and sat down, surrounded by aquatic sounds, unexpected splashing, no one would come in that night, he could've stretched out on a bench and slept until the next day if it wasn't so cold. He felt the tremble of the tracks and watched a light-laden train pass, reflected in the lake's dark water.

The train passed by, all lit up. In the sky was the balloon from that morning, with the two rays of helium stuck into its belly, like a big incandescent bulb illuminating the lake and filling the ground with shadows. There were also airplanes in flames. The lake was a burning pool. The fire had taken over the center of Sils, and the houses were aflame, the chimneys, the church tower with its red-hot bell. The isolated farm-houses in the woods and in the fields, and Miqui in his truck, and the cars passing by on the road and freeway. Infernos in the Guilleries and Montseny mountains, Vidreres ablaze, the streets, the homes, his parents, Iona; the limping bitch ran like a shadow between the flames with another dog, a dog whose fur was all burned, named Ringo. Nil hadn't heard anything from him since Saturday night when he lit him on fire and let him go, and the dog set off running like they all did, fleeing from himself through the fields. But something went wrong, because the flames went out, or it had only seemed they were going out, because that same fire was burning everything now, and Ringo was running, hairless, through it all, fleeing like he'd fled Saturday night, looking back every once in a while, farther and farther from Nil, until he crossed the road at the worst moment. Nil saw the lights, the *S* the car made, he heard the sudden braking, the shattering glass, he ran back to the shack to hide the fuel and the camera.

He touches his ear to make sure he's awake. Hell is here and he is the devil, but not everything can be destruction. He keeps walking and finds the Peugeot with Jaume and Xavi inside, two boys a bit younger than him, whom he'd met at some party in town.

"What are you two doing here?" he asks.

"Us?" says Jaume. "We're where we're supposed to be. And you, evil notary?"

He doesn't want to be that reincarnation. The water of the lake has to rise again, it has to drown the two boys, snuff out all the fires; or else it will all be hell.